Taichi:
The Story of a Chinese Master in America

A Novel

by

Marc Meyer

WARM WISHES TO
ANN KRANIS
BEST TO YOU ON
YOUR JOURNEY TO
HEALTH AND LONGEVITY

3/21/14

Taichi: The Story of a Chinese Master in America

Published by BookLocker.com, Inc., Bradenton, Florida.

Printed in the United States of America on acid-free paper.

The characters and events in this book are fictitious. Any similarity to real persons, living or dead, is coincidental and not intended by the author.

BookLocker.com, Inc.
2014

First Edition

Cover design: Todd Engel
Editor: Katia Vodin

Dedication

Dedicated to Ruth Lewin for all her love, generosity and support.

Chapter 1

Emerging from a bank of wet fog in the predawn hour, a merchant ship quietly chugged its way to a slip in New York Harbour with only a few family members and dockhands to greet it. Chinese families swarmed the decks from the stifling holds below, pressing their chests against the railings to catch a firsthand glimpse of this wondrous new land that cost many of them their savings and some their lives. Bedlam broke out almost immediately, as excited and frightened passengers scrambled to stay together, clutching at children and meagre possessions, which for some amounted only to a bag of sundries and a few pots and pans tied with string to their backs. Amidst all the shouting and mayhem stood a serene figure in a shabby brown raincoat and torn fedora. He was tall for a Chinese man, six feet, but possessed of a calm air and dignified manner that set him apart from his fellow travelers.

This was not my uncle's first trip to America. Thanks to one special visit accompanying the wife of Chiang Kai-Sheck as a personal bodyguard and two others in the service of the U.S. Ambassador to China, Uncle Kuo was in possession of one of those most rare and prized commodities in the Chinese world at the time of the Cultural Revolution, a diplomatic passport issued to him by the consulate in Beijing. He took no small pride in flashing the precious leather-bound item before the eyes of awestruck New York Customs officials.

Despite the important government titles my uncle held, he was a simple man who preferred to dress in plain peasant cloth with only a modest wool overcoat for protection against the elements and who often slept in steerage, which he called "fourth class," during voyages on Chinese steamer ships. His unassuming manner and no frills appearance belied the fact that he was also rumoured to be a descendant of royal blood through ancestral ties to the Manchurian courts. I thought he looked a bit past its expiration date, even sometime after he retired from public service, but for now, it was still valid. The customs agent greeted it with a suspiciously raised eyebrow, then waved him through impatiently and closed the gate behind him to a chorus of further protests. My uncle's head bowed ever lower to pick up his weather-beaten suitcase, but then his sweet face immediately brightened as he started to make a run towards us. He dropped his suitcase and reached out anxiously to hug my father and mother with his large hands. Then he turned to face my brother and I. Kuo grinned from ear to ear as he stood there, taking us in.

"Well well....look who we have here. These must be the two famous champions I've been hearing so much about!" We must have given each other such a funny look that it prompted everyone to start laughing.

"Come!" said Uncle, "Let's get out of here. I can't wait to sample those delectable noodles I know Mei has prepared for us." He gave us a huge smile with a wink and we felt his enormous hands on both of our shoulders, hustling us off the platform.

"I have brought all of you presents from Hong Kong, you will see," he said, grinning excitedly as we made a fast procession to the taxi stand for a taxi that would take us all back into Chinatown. My brother, Fa, and I remained unfazed by his enthusiasm. We had received gifts in the mail from Uncle Kuo before, and they had usually been cryptic type offerings, meant to instil some lasting moral values in us.

The taxi stand was jammed with uniformed porters blowing their whistles, shimmering yellow cabs, and a thousand people shouting for attention. My father put his hand on the door handle of one of the cabs before the driver could drive off and herded us all in. It was a tight squeeze with four of us in the car, but my younger brother, Fa, sat on my lap in the back seat, and we managed. My father got into the front seat and turned to the driver. "We are going to an address in Chinatown," he said.

Chapter 2

Once we got under way, my brother and I were pleased Kuo wasted no time in removing his famous fedora hat and showing it to us. He held it up from the inside with his fingertips and spun it around by the brim.

"This hat was once tailor made for me when I was a young man by the three most beautiful women in Hangzhou," he said, looking at it wistfully. "Unfortunately, it's not much to look at now." Fa and I glanced at each other and rolled our eyes, even as we clung to every word. We tried to picture the three beautiful young women, working diligently to produce the hat.

Soon we reached the outskirts of Chinatown and pulled up to the curb of a bustling intersection. The cab driver turned to us and announced, "That'll be ten dahllahs and fifty cents, Mack. Hope you got the fare." He looked at my father sceptically as if he was half expecting us to make a run for it. My father muttered something under his breath about highway robbery and the cabbie taking the scenic route, but he grabbed the man's hand, shoved eleven dollars into it and we all got out.

My parents lived in a fairly spacious two level apartment atop one of the oldest dry goods stores in Chinatown, a store which they owned and in which Fa and I helped most days after school. I worked there nights for part of my grade school years, most of my high school years, and even during a period of time spent deciding which college to attend. My mother christened me with the name Paul after one of the apostles, in hopes that it would enable me to fit in easier with my classmates and Western society in general. It was only after Fa came along that my parents realized we would still be subject to discrimination due to our Asian features. Everyone in my family called me "Paulie" and still do today.

"Paulie! Fa! Come! Help me set the table," called my mother from the kitchen, and we scurried to pick up the place a bit while our guest took a bath and freshened up.

Uncle Kuo soon appeared, still half wet in a large colourful silk kimono he had purchased in Japan. He paused, savouring the aromas emanating from my mother's steamy kitchen, then eagerly rubbed his hands together and winked at us. "Neither heaven nor earth could ever match the smell of your mother's cooking," he said softly. "Both should give up and admit their defeat." He was certainly right about that. To this day, I have never smelled or tasted anything as heavenly as my mother's delicate flat noodles smothered in a rich Hunan beef stew.

"Sit everyone!" she scolded, hurriedly bringing out steaming bowls of noodles and setting them at each place. My brother and I were starving, as was our new arrival, and none of us needed any encouragement.

"But Mei!" Uncle bellowed in protest. "I'm acting no better than a spoiled potentate being waited on hand and foot by coolies. Is there nothing I can do to make myself useful?"

"No, no," said my mother, sweetly patting my uncle back into his chair as he started to rise. "You look tired after that awful trip, and the sooner we get a nice hot meal into you, the better.

"Paulie," she said sternly, "get up and pour your uncle a glass of beer."

"No need to disturb the child, Mei. Expensive beer is too good for the likes of me. I am more than content with this fine New York City water fresh from the tap.

"Nonsense," said my mother. But I had already returned from the refrigerator with a bottle of Tsing Tao beer. Prying off the cap like an old pro, I held the glass up with my left hand and poured slowly with my right, the way my father had taught me. Uncle Kuo licked his lips and made a great show of being pleased, after which we slurped our noodles, joked, talked and laughed through a memorable dinner.

The evening was far from over to our pleasant surprise. Kuo had indeed purchased all of the family gifts in Hong Kong, and they would turn out to be more intriguing than we could possibly imagine. After dinner, the family retired to the living room for tea or, in some cases, to continue the conversation with the help of some hot Japanese sake.

"Time for me to show you your gifts," said Uncle Kuo, bounding up the flight of stairs like a cat and returning swiftly with his large peeling and gritty suitcase. He undid the straps and motioned us all to gather round. "For Mei..." he said with a playful smile, reaching in with both hands to grab a medium-sized, perfectly shaped, bamboo steamer.

My mother sat motionless on the sofa, her mouth agape, and feigning shock. She reached out and felt it all over with her hands admiringly as if she was trying to recapture some lost feeling of her homeland. "This is far too extravagant, Kuo. You shouldn't have."

"And have to go without my favourite dumplings?" he said, giving us such an exaggerated look that we all laughed.

Kuo had given Father his gifts earlier so he could enjoy them, some cigarettes from Hong Kong and a bottle of liquor from Shanghai. Now he turned to us with a mischievous smile. "Let's see, hmmmm..." he murmured, rummaging through some clothes with a puzzled expression. "Did I forget to bring something for my two champions? Hmmmmm, that's funny... must have left it behind."

Fa and I looked at each other miserably; our hearts sank. By now we could have wished for anything to make an appearance from that old suitcase, a scarf perhaps, or even a pair of socks. Then Uncle hid a smile, and we knew he was up to his old tricks. "Aha!" he exclaimed triumphantly. "Here it was all along. I knew it."

He reached down to the very bottom, pulled out two square cut pieces of brocade cloth that resembled hanging tapestries, and laid them both out end to end. Thinking at first that this was something meant to enhance the decor of our rooms, both Fa and I forced ourselves to look as pleased as possible. Then we fairly jumped out of our seats as uncle gingerly unwrapped the cloth. There, gleaming before our very eyes, lay two exquisite double-edged jian swords, the jewels of the Chinese military and martial artist alike. Both were perfect miniature replicas. Kuo leaned back in his chair, relishing our expressions.

"Better be careful with those things, kids," said my mother, giving Uncle Kuo a smile couched in a slightly disapproving look.

"Remember now, boys, at present these are only for decoration. One day I will teach you how to train with them. But until that day comes...," said our uncle holding up a warning finger.

We got the message but of course couldn't resist wielding them at each other just a bit until my mother's sharp glance told us to stop. "You'll break everything in the house!" she wailed. "Take those swords upstairs, wrap them back in their covers, and put them on top of the cedar chest in the hall where your father and I can keep an eye on them."

"Boys will be boys, Mei..." Kuo started in, but Mom put up a hand to silence him. This was her house, and she was damned if she was going to let her two young ruffians dismantle it.

My father gave us a look that said he would dismantle *us* if we didn't do exactly what our mother said. "You indulge them far too much, Kuo," said my stepfather in a serious tone. "Tomorrow's a school day and it's past bedtime for you two. Say goodnight, and you better be in bed by the time I get upstairs."

Fa and I shuffled up the staircase in unison, toward the dark shadows, listening to the sounds of my stepfather and our new guest chuckling and toasting each other into the night. We obediently laid our two prize possessions on top of the chest of drawers in the hallway, turned the lights out in our room, and pretended to go to sleep.

Of course, we were much too excited to do so and found ourselves lying face up with arms folded behind our heads, eyes wide open. We chatted for awhile about the day's events and then listened to the sounds in the house as they slowly died away. I probably fell asleep at the same time as Fa, but I've always been a light sleeper and was enticed back into consciousness by some muffled footsteps coming from my room, the room which was newly occupied by Uncle Kuo for the duration of his visit. The footsteps were as light as those of a cat and made me wonder at first if someone had brought an animal into the house. I climbed out of bed and stole as quietly as a commando down the hall toward the door. The door was open a crack, and I could see the yellow light of my room boring through it. I pressed my face against the crack. Kuo was still up, engaged in some sort of odd dance, waving his hands about and moving lightly from side to side, first on one foot, then the other. After several minutes watching him, I grew bored and returned to bed, reasoning that this was just another in a series of mysterious pastimes for which our unusual guest was well known.

I was dreaming I was a tree, being vigorously shaken by forest gnomes to release its fruit, when I heard my mother's voice close to my ear. She was shaking me by the shoulders, "Paulie...hurry up now...get up! There is no one coming in to open the store this morning, and I need your help." It was still dark, and I could hear Fa softly breathing over in the next bed, fast asleep.

Some time in the late 1930's, my stepfather traded in his Chinese first name for Harold and was henceforth known as "Harry" Chen. Harry Chen bought the family's dry goods store and the property above it from my real father, who left my brother and I when we were still in our cribs. Precious little information was shared with us about our original father other than the fact that he had suddenly decided one day to enlist in the army, declaring that he was going to fight for Japan, and never returned. My brother and I pictured him as a kind of nutty war hero, but we always looked up to Harry Chen as our real father. I inched my way, half asleep with flashlight in hand, down the rickety stairs to the basement and flipped on the circuit breakers.

Our dry goods store dated back to the 1800's, and mother and father did their best to uphold some of its venerable traditions. They occasionally extended credit to some of the more regular customers, and one could still stumble across the odd bag of horse feed, once kept in great quantities in the storerooms to be administered to carriage horses.

While helping my mother tidy up the counters and fill the displays, I could hear Fa getting dressed over my head. I threw a sandwich together and stuffed it into a paper bag. Then picking up the remainder of my things for school, I wondered aloud if I should take my new sword with me to show the other kids.

"You are *not* taking that sword to school, Paulie," my mother snapped. "You are going to act responsibly and set an example for your younger brother, even if your uncle seems incapable of doing so." I grabbed a piece of nougat from one of the antique glass jars, bit off the end, and munched away as I waited for Fa.

At last, my brother made a woozy appearance at the top of the stairwell, weaving back and forth, sword in hand like a drunken, conquering hero. "Ah ah! I'll take that," said Mom firmly, holding out her hand. Fa pursed his lips and gave her a mournful look, but Mother was all too well acquainted with my brother's pallet of wilful emotions, and it failed to meet its mark. He looked at me for support, but all I could do was shrug helplessly.

Asian women could be very tough, and my mother was no exception. We shouldered our book bags, and she gave us a quick kiss on the foreheads. Then we waved goodbye, setting off through a light snow to the bus stop in silence.

14

Chapter 3

Uncle Kuo hit the deck about noon. He was lucky. Only minor damages had been inflicted by the previous night's debauchery. There were some awkward, drunken moments when he tried unsuccessfully to make a good impression on his estranged sister. Everything was fixable, he decided, but first he would need a steaming cup of black coffee, heavily laden with sugar to warm his chilled bones, and then one of those strong Chinese cigarettes from Hong Kong. Afterward, he would somehow formulate a plan to make himself useful to the entire family for the rest of the day.

He donned his kimono and started gingerly down the staircase steps. "Mei?" he called out tentatively. "Mei!"

"Oh hi, brother," said Mom, peering from the entrance to the kitchen and giving him a playful smile. "Sleep well?"

"Like a horrible old black bear," he grunted.

Mom laughed. "I left some coffee on for you. It's a bit old but still nice and hot."

"Mei, you are a saint," he said, "placed here on earth to brighten our days. I was unbelievably exhausted. Thanks for letting me sleep in today; I can't believe it's so late."

"That's quite all right, dear brother. We tried to be quiet, but you know how it is with two kids. Anyway, it's always nice to see *someone* getting some sleep around here."

Kuo nodded solemnly, "I know what you mean." He poured some coffee into a cup left for him on the counter and drew a cigarette discreetly from its pack. "Harry get off all right this morning?"

"Yes, fine," said Mei, "he's been at work for hours."

Kuo took his coffee upstairs and out to the second floor porch where he gulped it down and lit a cigarette. The porch afforded a spectacular view of the Chinatown streets, and Kuo breathed it all in with a resounding sigh of satisfaction. After a few minutes, Mei overheard him talking on the telephone.

"Hello, Jimmy! Yes, yes it's me...can you come by here now? What? Do you know the address? Yes, yes fine, I'll meet you out front.

"A friend from the old days, Jimmy Chow, is picking me up, Mei," Kuo announced. "We are having lunch, and then he is going to help me open an account at the bank and scout out some locations for the school. I thought you might want me do some food shopping for you at the market before we return."

Mei looked at him with the reaction he was hoping for, a mixture of relief and gratitude. "That would be good of you, thanks Kuo. I'll leave a list on the kitchen table."

"It'll be just like old times," said Uncle, smiling broadly at her. Kuo was a long-time, ardent fan of my mother's cooking and often went to the market to buy fruits and vegetables for her when the family lived in China.

Once there, he took his time, shopping among the colourful produce, taking in the sweet smells, and listening to the conversations of people from the countryside recounting their miseries. It was among these people that he first heard the term "martial artist", listening to stories about mythical figures who roamed the countryside, fighting as if magically possessed.

Today, however, there would be no dilly-dallying, and Kuo was furious at himself for having slept so late. He paced back and forth next to the storefront on the slushy sidewalk, stamping his feet and rubbing his hands to ward off the cold. Each day spent in America as Harry Chen's guest was precious, and he reminded himself to value that time as his future plans relied heavily on it. He paced some more, waiting for Jimmy Chow. Finally, a car horn sounded across the street. Uncle pulled up the collar of his overcoat and ran toward it.

Jimmy was a tough but lovable friend of the family's who spent most of his twenties as a Shanghai policeman. Kuo had been teaching T'ai Chi at the police academy when they first met, and Jimmy always admired the way he could throw two hundred pound men around effortlessly, like pieces of cotton. In fact, Jimmy had the highest respect for Kuo, both as a friend and as a formidable martial arts master. He would do anything for my uncle at the drop of a hat, spending entire days helping him out and running errands whenever called upon.

Jimmy rolled down his window and chuckled as he watched Kuo's large, bony frame running across the street. Uncle reached in the window and gave him a hug. Jimmy threw open the passenger door and Kuo leaped in.

"Not even one day here and I'm restless already," grumbled Kuo. "Mei has turned into my mother." They both doubled up with laughter.

Jimmy Chow drove straight to Chase Manhattan Bank where Kuo, with the aid of some official documents, managed to open two accounts set up to receive transferred funds from Hong Kong. He chafed a bit at his friend's newly acquired citizenship. Jimmy became a naturalized U.S. citizen a scant three months before Kuo's arrival in New York, thanks to his American birth mother. He spoke better English than Kuo and had thus ascended to a higher stature in their relationship.

Kuo applied to the State Department to grant him citizenship through his diplomatic ties, but he knew this could take several months, and there were no guarantees. Still, he emerged from the Chase Manhattan building with a satisfied smile.

"I can already feel the keys to my new studio in my hands," he gloated.

Jimmy smiled, knowing there would be endless hurdles to come, but patted his friend's back encouragingly. "Now I have something to show you; I've found the perfect place," said Jim.

Chapter 4

The studio was located in a run down section of the East Village. The room had been a school for classically trained danseuses in the early forties. Its shabby mirrors and stained wood floors once played host to ballet teachers the likes of Martha Graham and Marie Harkness. Buried beneath a decade of old dust, the place cried out to be restored to its former usefulness. Kuo ran his index finger over one of the large interior windowsills. "This place is perfect, Jim. How on earth did you find it?"

"I've been waiting for you to see it for weeks," said his friend, leaning against the door frame and watching Uncle with an amused smile. Come, let's talk about it over lunch. How long has it been since you saw the inside of a real deli?"

"Long enough," said Kuo, laughing and putting an arm around Jimmy's shoulders. Both men started down the street, smiling and chatting, when out of the corner of his eye, Kuo suddenly became aware of a commotion.

At first it appeared as if two women were having an argument in a back alley, but as the taller one turned around, Kuo was shocked to see a man with a full grown beard. He looked at Jim quizzically who could only shrug in return. "Hey, guys are wearing their hair long these days; what can I tell you?" he said.

The commotion grew louder as the longhaired man, turning out to be an assailant, grabbed his victim by the hair and started reaching for her purse. At that moment, a second man appeared, grabbing both the victim's arms and pulling them behind her back.

"Let the woman go... now!" shouted Kuo, coming up fast on the taller of the two men with Jim only inches behind.

"Who do you think you're messing with, old man?" sneered the brute, whirling around to face him. He threw a punch that missed Kuo's face by inches. Kuo grabbed part of his hand in a joint lock that brought him instantly to his knees and then kicked him lightly in the stomach, knocking the wind out of him. The longhaired man's partner watched in astonishment. Grabbing the two men by the backs of their jackets, Kuo gave each a hard shove, sending them flying down the street. The men slunk off together, looking over their shoulders.

"Who would have pegged *him* for a brawler?" asked the shorter man.

"Shut up," said his friend between gasps of breath, "I think he's looking for property around here. Don't worry, we'll see him again."

The men gave another glance over their shoulders then turned and walked off. Jimmy clapped his hands together and laughed. "Master, I can see that you have lost none of your skill," he warbled. Kuo waved the compliment aside and asked the woman if she was all right.

"Yes...yes," she said breathlessly. "Thank you!" giving him a big hug. Then she clutched at her purse and ran down the street.

Kuo watched her disappear from sight. "Now I'm hungry," he said, looking at his watch, "and we'll have to hurry. I promised Mei I'd do some shopping for her."

On the bus ride home, Fa leaned in and said in a conspiratorial whisper, "What was all that about last night?"

"What do you mean?" I said, pretending to be ignorant.

"I saw you spying on old Kuo in the hallway."

"I did no such thing," I said. "I simply saw a light on and went to investigate."

"You sure about that?" said Fa with a tone that warned me I could be blackmailed about this at some future date. He was, after all, one of the most respected nine year olds in his field. I dropped it and stared out the window for the remainder of the bus ride.

Uncle Kuo beat us home by minutes. We stumbled upon him washing vegetables in the kitchen sink and held our breath. Fa put a finger up to his lips, and we tried to sneak quietly upstairs to our bedrooms before he caught sight of us, but it was too late.

"Paulie! Fa! In here!" he bellowed over running water. We dropped our book bags at the foot of the stairs and dragged ourselves to the kitchen. Kuo was hacking through the end of a large purple rutabaga with a heavy cleaver.

"We have homework, Uncle," I protested, knowing that he was about to turn us into prep cooks for the better part of the evening.

"Boys, here are two sharp knives," he said, ignoring my plea. "Fa, you take the carrots, and Paulie, you take the potatoes. Set them on the cutting board, and peel them in the wastebasket over there."

I started to open my mouth with another excuse, but something about seeing him standing there insistently with a meat cleaver changed my mind. Like it or not, we would be helping to make preparations for my mother's Szechuan vegetable soup.

"Now, you two be careful of those knives; they're very sharp," he said. My little brother looked up at me in disgust. I had failed to save him from his fate and as a result felt like a miserable failure myself.

"Come on!" said Uncle. "Quick! You know, in my great-grandfather's time, farm implements and cooking utensils were used as weapons." Fa rolled his eyes. Oh no, not another lecture on top of this. What could be worse? My stepfather, that's what could be worse. Within minutes, Harry Chen's booming voice entered the kitchen.

"Evening everyone!" He kissed us and patted our heads. "What a big help you are to your mother, boys," he said, then turned to our new tormentor.

"Come, Kuo, this is woman's work. Come out to the living room with me and have a beer." Kuo managed to hold forth with a couple of weak protests, but eventually succumbed to the large T.V. recliner in the living room. They sat and talked for a few minutes, sipping their beers. Fa and I listened in on the conversation.

"Well, Uncle," said my stepfather, "you look different somehow. Have you had a profitable day or a troublesome one?"

"Life, dear brother-in-law, is always Yin and Yang, as we both know," said Kuo, chuckling.

"And the school," said Harry, "any luck?"

Kuo's mind flashed back to the moment he was standing by the second floor window of the studio, looking out toward the alleyway where the fight would occur within minutes. There was something troubling about the location he couldn't shake, a strong feeling that this place was a haven for dangerous individuals of every sort. "Jimmy has found the perfect place for me," he said.

Shortly after Fa and I left the kitchen to do our homework, Mei came back to a mountain of chopped and peeled vegetables. She hugged my uncle exuberantly, almost spilling his beer.

"Oh thank you, loveable brother...." she began, making him blush.

"Now wait, Mei. Everything would have been a complete disaster had it not been for my two hard working assistants over there," he said, pointing to my brother and I coming down the stairs.

You can say that again, I thought to myself.

"Thanks, kids," said my mother, hugging the stuffing out of us. "Dinner will be ready soon. Harry, since you have managed to avoid all this work, I give you the honour of setting the table."

"My pleasure, Mei," he said, laughing. "Although I have been waiting on your brother hand and foot like an old coolie ever since I got in." Uncle thumbed his nose at Harry and gave him a big raspberry, which made us all laugh. After two bowls of spicy, hot soup each and pieces of bread warmed by the oven, Uncle had an announcement to make.

"Boys, you've done a splendid job helping to prepare this fine meal for us. Tonight, I am going to give you your first lesson on the finer points of Chinese swordsmanship." Sensing my mother's rising apprehension, he cupped his hand over his mouth and finished, "Upstairs on the porch. My brother and I quickly excused ourselves and headed upstairs, closely followed by my Uncle.

"Fetch your swords, gentlemen. Let's see yours, Paulie," he said, snatching the sword lightly out of my hand as if it had been picked up by a sudden wind. He held up the handle level with his nose and looked straight down the blade. "Hmmm..." he said, then bounced the sword around in his right hand a bit, feeling its weight. "This will do. Do either of you boys know the parts which make up a sword?" he asked. Fa and I shook our heads in unison. "This is the pommel," he said, pointing to the tip of the handle. "It's the top part which screws the hilt and handle to the blade."

"And what are these silly things for?" asked Fa, wiggling his fingers through the braids of two tassels hanging from the sword.

"The tassel," replied Uncle," is used to distract the enemy the same way a magician uses a pretty assistant to distract the observer at precisely the right moment.

"And this," he said, "is the hilt, which protects the hand from the opposing blade." Then holding the sword lightly, palm up in his right hand, he began to move slowly from one foot to the other. "Wandering through a string of pearls or pulling a silk thread from its cocoon are the things we use to describe the movement of Taichi," he said.

Fa and I giggled at first, but we continued to watch as our old uncle managed to transform himself into a being of lightness and grace, a supple yet fierce looking animal that seemed ready to pounce at any minute. After showing us some basic steps from the Taichi sword routine, Uncle sat on the porch steps leading out from the doorway. He lit a cigarette and watched. In this manner, master Kuo Yun San taught us an hour each day for the three months he remained our houseguest.

Chapter 5

By the following November, Kuo had accomplished much. His English had improved. He had his citizenship papers, a small apartment in Queens, and a school with a burgeoning roster of students. Jimmy Chow was brought on board as assistant coach along with a slice of a girl named Ba Ling.

Ba Ling, or "Ling Ling," as the students nicknamed her, was a seventeen year old transfer student from Beijing who immigrated to the U.S. through Ellis Island. She was reputed to have been a star of the Beijing Wushu Team at a very young age. The term "wushu" is similar to the word "Kung Fu" used by many Westerners to describe Chinese martial arts.

Ling Ling was slender, to the point of being anorexic, with a long dancer's neck and luxurious black hair reaching halfway down her back which she wore in a ponytail. She had the most perfect skin, eyes, ears, and nose I had ever seen, and I was smitten with her immediately.

Jimmy Chow had been on her trail ever since she moved to New York. He wasted no time introducing her to Kuo and recommending that she be hired as a member of his teaching staff. Needless to say, my uncle's male students were thrilled, and couldn't resist showing off whenever she was around.

I was happy for the few stolen moments that enabled me to catch a glimpse of her stretching or working out before a class. I was afforded these rare moments only when Fa and I were allowed visits to the studio or asked to run the occasional errand for my uncle. I considered it a privilege to watch her sword routine, which paired a kind of lethal femininity with artistic grace.

Jimmy Chow, my uncle, and Ling Ling began to spend a lot of time around each other and it wouldn't be long before they formed a close association. Slowly, Ling Ling was wooed into the bosom of my family like an adopted sibling. To this day, my wife has exhibited a jealous streak towards her, though Ling Ling is quite a bit older and my marriage a happy one with three children. She took on extra classes for my uncle, backed him through thick and thin, and I suppose there were times when she and I grew close, though nothing ever came of it.

"Remember!" my uncle would call out as we watched him lead a class. "Upper body like a butterfly's wings, legs like steel. Remember to practice stillness within the movement!" The art and practice of T'ai Chi struck a resounding chord in the Sixties with the young holistic set. As a result, my uncle found his studio flooded with longhairs, beatniks, radicalists, and cultists of every sort. Looking out onto the sea of beads and beards, he often wondered if he was getting through to them. He hoped so. He wanted to be a kind of mental therapy for them. God knows they needed it.

Kuo was generous with his time, letting some of them slide on their fees if he knew things were tough at home. He spent extra amounts of time late at night with the more gifted ones, driving them home if they needed a ride. He drove groups of them to our dry goods store in Chinatown, explaining the medicinal qualities of certain Chinese herbs, showing them some of Mei's calligraphy, which he admired very much, or telling them the story of Yang Luchan.

It was at these times Fa and I would invariably be caught and recognized working in our aprons, which was always the height of humiliation for us. Uncle acted as if he keenly enjoyed the entire event, our humiliation included. He made a grand commotion of pulling out chairs and barrels for everyone to sit on, then took great delight in seating us front and center among his best looking female students, beaming with satisfaction at our discomfort and flushed complexions. Fa and I exchanged angry glances at these moments. Who did be think he was anyway? Did he think he owned the place and could give impromptu lectures any time he felt like it? We seethed at the colossal ego and pomposity of the man but decided not to utter a word. Instead we listened obediently to the story of Yang Luchan while the pungent store odours invaded our nostrils. I can name them all to this day.

"The story of Yang style Taichi begins in a place very much like this," Kuo started in, looking around for emphasis and supporting his back against the sales counter.

"Well, perhaps a bit smaller because Hopei, centuries ago, was a very poor province in Eastern China. In fact, the place looked more like what you would call an apothecary today with hundreds more medicine jars than you could find here. It was called the Hall of Great Harmony. Its proprietor was one of the wealthiest men in town, and the man he hired to run it was one of the greatest Taichi fighters in the country.

"One day, a sick young man by the name of Yang Luchan wandered into the store, looking for a cure, and found two men arguing. A very big customer was yelling at the manager, complaining that the prices were too high. After a few minutes, the manager came out from behind the counter, and with very little effort, threw the customer from the back of the store out into the middle of the street, where he was almost hit by a fast horse." Everyone always giggled at that one. Kuo continued. "Yang was amazed at what he saw, and asked the manager if he would teach him anything about this wonderful martial art. The man hired Yang as a servant, but because he was not a family member, refused to teach him anything." From here Uncle meandered on through the long-winded account of Yang Luchan's life, about how Yang did menial work for the household, biding his time patiently, until one night, he heard yelling coming from one of the buildings next door.

He climbed up the building, peeled off a section of the plaster, and looked through a hole, revealing a training hall filled with practicing martial artists. Each evening, Yang secretly climbed the wall, peered through the hole, memorized everything he saw, and practiced late into the night while everyone slept. Within a few years, he became so accomplished he was able to challenge his employer's family members to a fight, soundly beating them all. After a few more demonstrations, his employer was flabbergasted and angry, knowing that Yang had spied on them. Yet he had to admit that Yang's skills were better than any of his family members and let the young man study with him for ten years.

Following this long and gruelling apprenticeship, Yang Luchan traveled to Peking to demonstrate his Taichi at a large banquet given for the emperor. When the emperor saw he was poorly dressed and small in stature, he sat him at a place reserved for the least well respected of his guests. Yang quietly for his turn as the match got underway. His opponent, a known champion who had beaten everyone else in the tournament, rushed at him with both fists. Yang sucked in his chest a bit, then seemed to just tap the upper part of his opponent's hand. The opponent shot like a bullet past Yang to the other side of the room, falling with his fists still clenched in the same position. The emperor was impressed and seated Yang Luchan in a place of honour reserved for his highest ranking guests. From that point on, everyone referred to him as "Yang the Invincible."

"Yang Luchan passed on his methods to his sons and it is their version of the art that we are learning today," Uncle finished up to general smiles and some light applause. This had often been my mother's cue to bring in a tray of some baked goods and candies from the store rooms to pass around to the grateful flower children, some of whom looked as though they hadn't eaten in days. Kuo took the opportunity to introduce Mei as a woman of many talents pointing out the delicate brushstrokes of her calligraphy adorning the walls.

Occasionally, Jimmy Chow and Ling Ling joined the assembly to my further chagrin and embarrassment. I still had a deep crush on Ling Ling and longed to converse with her in private anywhere but that store. Whenever Uncle finished telling one of his stories in front of a group, both Ling Ling and Jimmy looked up at him and smiled knowingly. Fa and I surmised that they had grown up with similar legends as kids at a time when they probably held more appeal. I remember being riveted by the stories in his letters when my brother and I were much younger, and I have continued the tradition of re- telling them for students of mine to this day. We particularly enjoyed tales of the Shaolin warrior monks. They contained a child's treasure trove of heroes, emperors, sword fights, superhuman feats of strength, the weak overcoming the strong, and training methods unthinkable to the average human being, all conveniently wrapped up in life lessons and supposed first-hand accounts of the temple by Uncle Kuo. The one that stood out most in my mind was about a certain Buddhist priest. The third son of a Brahmin Indian King named Bodhidharma.

Bodhidharma left India as a Buddhist missionary, crossing the Himalayas in 526 A.D., and beginning a pilgrimage that would bring him to the gates of the Shaolin, or "Little Forest," temple in Henan China. When he came across the monks at Shaolin, he found them busy at their desks, transcribing ancient Sanskrit into Chinese. He also found them weak, unhealthy, and malnourished from hours of seated meditation and a general lack of physical activity. Thereupon, he immediately prescribed an exercise regimen known as the Luohan, a set of eighteen exercises based on the movements of animals. The bear, snake, tiger, leopard and crane formed the inspiration behind these movements, which became known as the five animal forms.

Gradually through a long period of time, the Shaolin monks developed a fighting system from this exercise into what is now more commonly known as Kung Fu. Kung Fu, the literal translation of which implies skill through effort, uses the five animals' exercises as different strategies for dealing with an opponent. The monks regained their health, and from that day forward, Bodhidharma became an icon. His fame spread throughout Asia, and many likenesses were created of him, one of which had been engraved into the hilt of our swords.

It was still the early sixties in America, however. Bruce Lee movies were a decade away, and Kung Fu was only taught secretly among a few small enclaves of America's Chinatowns. The reaction of our school chums to Uncle Kuo's stories was generally laughter and derision, even though his sudden apparitions in a kimono often scared the life out of them. Tall, broad-shouldered, and fierce looking with sword in hand, my uncle could have been a page from a history book come to life. A momentary glimpse of him was enough to send schoolmates scattering out of the store and down the block, to our wild delight.

For students seeking knowledge at the hard-working altar of Chinese martial arts, Kuo had the exact opposite effect. They flocked to him, worshiped him, and followed him around, clinging to his every word until he dismissed them with a wave of his hand and a curt farewell.

"I have business; find something to do," he would tell them irritably, then grab Jimmy Chow and Ling Ling and start walking in the opposite direction. If one of them lingered, he would turn around and yell "Go!" until they disappeared.

By evening, it would narrow down to the three of them. Uncle, Jimmy Chow and Ling Ling poured into the streets, laughing and chatting with each other until late into the night. The unlikely trio would be recognized here and there, dropping in on friends unannounced with bottles of sake in hand. Fa and I sometimes called them the three stooges when we were feeling spiteful, but since uncle refused to own a radio or T.V set, he never quite caught on. He always gave a suspicious look whenever we said it that sent us into peals of laughter. I dared not make fun of Ling Ling in her presence. I revered this stunning example of young womanhood and gave withering looks at anyone who even disagreed with her. I would have done anything for her; all she had to do was ask. She only asked once. Actually, it was more of a command.

Fa and I had just entered the studio for a visit when I heard her call, "Stand back!" from the other side of the room. The sharp blade of a broadsword whooshed by my arm, narrowly missing it. Ling Ling deftly caught the assailant's hand with a light smack, bringing him to the ground and disarming him within seconds. Then I watched with awe and horror as the student put his arm around her and they both ran laughing out into the hallway, kissing on the lips.

Flushed and shaken, I stood there embarrassed, not knowing what do with myself until Uncle predictably shook me out of my reverie. "Nephew!" he shouted, "Come over here." Seeing the miserable state I was in, he put his arm around me and said softly, "I'm sorry, Nephew. You are becoming a young man, and as you get older, you will see that life doesn't always play fair. Yet sometimes we have to try to accept it with dignity and grace. Now go to the store and get me two quarts of chocolate ice cream. You and Fa can keep one of them for yourselves, and tell Mei I've released you from duty for the rest of the afternoon."

I looked up at him with tears in my eyes and gave him a hug. He always knew the right thing to say. "Thanks, Uncle," I snivelled into his enormous wool overcoat. Then I grabbed Fa by the sleeve, and we raced downstairs and out the door towards the ice cream shop.

Chapter 6

As usual, Kuo's instincts about the alleyway running up the side of the building where he taught proved correct. It was a place well known throughout the neighbourhood as a haven for men or beasts down on their luck. One afternoon Ling Ling and Jimmy Chow finished up classes early, and Uncle sought to reward their efforts by taking them out to dinner. They closed up shop, and with arms around each other, headed down the street to a favourite neighbourhood restaurant of Kuo's choosing. As they passed the alleyway behind the building, Kuo became acutely aware of a menacing presence following them with its eyes. Suddenly, a large pit bull shot out of the alley and dove off the sidewalk with a roar and went straight for Ling Ling's throat. Quick as lightening, Uncle stepped in front of Ling Ling, catching the dog squarely below the jaw with his foot and sending him flying through the air. The dog subsequently fell and collapsed dead on the pavement.

"I hated doing that," said Kuo, feeling shaken. He was very mindful of animals and critical of anyone who he thought treated them poorly.

"Is everyone all right?" he asked.

Ling Ling nodded along with Jimmy. She was breathing hard with her hands up around her throat. "My reactions..." she began but Uncle cut her off.

"Don't worry, you didn't see him." He knelt by the animal feeling for a pulse. "This was a very troubled old fellow," he said, softly patting the creature's back. "He's better off asleep".

The dog turned out to be a stray. The trio walked back to the studio in solemn silence. Jimmy called a canine unit to have the animal picked up. Ling Ling excused herself and went to the bathroom. Lowering his voice Jimmy turned to my uncle and said, "You must teach her the Dalu."

Kuo put up a hand to silence him. "All in good time, Jim," he said. Ling Ling re-emerged, her gorgeous, elegant self. "Come," said Kuo, "let's have a nice dinner before it gets too late."

The Dalu gives the illusion of a slow hypnotic dance between two partners. Deeply hidden beneath the surface is a sophisticated component of the martial art Taichi that involves attacking and defending the four corners. They would be equivalent to the half cardinal points on a compass: SE. SW. NE. and NW. Kuo usually taught these sophisticated techniques to a student last, say after about five to ten years of training. Ling Ling had some background and showed some talent and, oddly after tonight, some weakness in her training. Uncle began to take more of a personal hand in the development of her skills. In order to bring her up to speed, he taught her the Dalu at night in the courtyard around the back of his studio, preferably when there was moonlight. Fa and I sometimes stopped by on our bicycles to watch.

For an instant, Uncle would become as young and graceful as Ling Ling. They shadowed each other in the moonlight, a slow tangle of arms and feet. The neighbours, perhaps understandably, grew concerned about all the goings on in the "weirdo building" across the street. They were becoming suspicious of the longhaired bearded types who came and went all hours of the day, and it was feared that some kind of mystic or satanic cult might be brewing right under their noses. Groups of hippies were seen performing impossibly slow, trance-like movements that were as yet unfamiliar and could be disturbing to those inclined to misinterpret them. The local inhabitants weren't sure what to make of it, but either way, some of them didn't much like it. Eventually, someone called the police.

Kuo was no stranger to clashes with authorities over the practice of his art; he had experienced the same thing in China. He accepted it as a normal by-product of people's ignorance and found that he could always handle the situation politely while firmly standing his ground. Uncle did not hesitate or miss a single step leading his group as he watched a detachment of five police officers, hands on their billy clubs, crossing the street and making their way over to the courtyard. He motioned the group to stop and ordered everyone to stand behind him. He then walked over toward the man he guessed to be the highest ranking of the bunch.

"Is der ah problem officers?" he said, making no attempt to disguise his Chinese accent.

"The problem is, this looks like an unlawful assembly," replied the sergeant, tapping a billy club in the palm of his left hand to make sure Kuo got the message. Kuo could have received an Oscar nomination for the wounded look he gave back to the officer.

"Me? Do something against the law?" he said meekly, putting his hand over his chest. "I would never..."

"Then what's going on here?" interrupted the sergeant. "Who are you and what are you up to?"

"I am master Kuo Yun San, an American citizen," said Uncle. "These are my students and this..." he said pointing up to the room on the second floor, "is my studio."

"Well, we've had complaints about all the traffic coming and going out of here," said the sergeant. "What are you a master of exactly?"

"Sir, I am a teacher of T'ai Chi Chuan."

"A what!?" asked the sergeant, cutting Kuo off in mid-sentence. "I'll need to see your permits and citizenship papers." Turning to the contingent of officers behind him, he chuckled. "Please."

"I will be glad to," my uncle told him, "but first give me leave to dismiss my students who are attending other classes at the university."

The sergeant thought for a while scratching his head then relented. "Well, all right, but we may want to talk to some of you later. For now you can go. All right, master whatever your name is, let's go," he said, waving the officers into the building and up the stairs behind Kuo. Of course, everything was found to be in order. Uncle Kuo was meticulous about everything, including the records of his students.

Of my uncle's students, it could be said that most were decent, kind, and good-natured. To their credit, many of them worked very hard and managed to stay with him for a number of years. He rewarded those who showed the most diligence by passing on his most carefully guarded secrets.

There was one core group consisting of five individuals that Kuo jokingly named after the five philosophical Chinese earthly elements: wood, fire, metal, earth, and water. The nicknames stuck with the students because Kuo named them based on appearances.

There was "Water," a shy young girl whose last name was really Waterman. Sally Waterman was a poor, teenage, Jewish girl from Brooklyn who came from a broken home. She joined the growing rank of students who showed promise but rarely shelled out a dime for class. Like the others, she worshipped my uncle and would do anything for him. For him, this was often enough, but Jimmy Chow wound up shaking his head in disgust.

"Let this mother of hers pay us something," he grumbled, writing out another cheque from the dwindling reserves.

Kuo waved him off. "She'll pay us when she can."

Her boyfriend, "Fire," so named because of his flaming red hair, often settled Sally's accounts with Kuo behind her back, then missed some payments of his own.

Uncle was lenient. He knew most of the students were from local colleges, doing the best they could with their parents' allowances.

"Metal, Wood, and Earth," were as different from each other as night and day. Metal was a muscle-bound metallurgist and steel worker who spent much of his day in the company of a welding torch. Wood, sometimes known as "Tree," was thin as a rail and tall as a sequoia tree. "Earth," or "Earth Mother," as she was sometimes known, was a dyed-in-the-wool hippy woman in her fifties. Earth Mother had a boutique where she sewed together her original "creations" out of second hand clothes.

Metal, or Tom, which was his real name, spent most of his free time in an old aircraft hangar welding large metal sculptures together into enormous jagged ones that seemed ready to punch a hole in the ceiling. One could become slack jawed just gazing up at the sheer immensity of these things. I remember once when he invited a group of us including my little brother and Uncle Kuo over one afternoon to see his work.

Fa gripped my fingers nervously, fearing that one of these mountainous structures might collapse on us any minute. I had to admit, the sight of all that jagged metal made me uneasy as well, but I put on a mature act, walking around the pieces as if I was appraising them for their artistic value.

Metal entertained us by showing off the two most important tools of his trade. We saw our reflections as he flipped down the visor on his helmet and looked on with silent awe as he lit the welding torch with a thump. A long blue flame darted toward the floor, and sparks flew off the tip with a crackle, missing us by inches. When it was over, my uncle thanked him, offering some words of quiet praise and patted him on the shoulder.

Chapter 7

Weather permitting, Uncle would occasionally take his students to a nearby park. He preferred to lead the procession in the misty morning hours when the pink sun rose between the buildings. People were catching their last precious hours of sleep and policemen sipped coffee before an early morning shift. Passersby gawked at the rows of people standing eerily still, casting long shadows between the trees.

Their arms were outstretched as if hugging someone or something invisible to their chests. It was an exercise in standing meditation, known as Chi -Kung, a method of building internal strength whereby an individual in a relaxed standing position could allow his chi, or life force, to circulate unobstructed through his body. Shaolin monks were made to stand for hours in these gruelling meditative postures that were the benefactors of health and martial potency.

Uncle paced back and forth in front of the group. "Pretend you are holding a large tree," he called out. "Now drop your elbows and your shoulders and just relax, breathe as you were shown earlier. When I was a very young student at the temple in Hangzhou, I once asked my teacher, a great master, why we were made to stand in this way. He told us to observe a tree, still on the outside but inside there is much activity."

In two quick strides he was over to where Tree was holding his position, putting a hand on his shoulder. "Like this tree here," he said, which caused everyone to break out into a smile, except for Tree who was very serious and took life very seriously. Tree was always breaking up with one girlfriend or another. Life was an internal battlefield for him and he looked as if he was in constant turmoil. My uncle persistently, and sometimes annoyingly, quoted him passages from the Tao Te Ching in an attempt to help him smooth out his life by taking a different view of it. Whether this approach ever helped, no one knew, but Tree revered my uncle so much he patiently listened to anything he had to say.

Earth Mother decided the group looked a little shabby and took it upon herself to ask Uncle Kuo if she could make some uniforms for them. Kuo was dead set against it at first because he always taught his students that uniforms were not needed for Taichi and that Chinese everywhere practiced in their street clothes. Also, due to his recent confrontation with the police, he felt no desire to attract any further attention. After some persuasion on the part of Earth Mother, however, he finally relented, only because he knew she was a well-meaning, kind, and nurturing woman who loved his classes and who felt that she would be making a much-needed contribution. Perhaps she was right. After all, the group could certainly use a little spiffing up. Even Fa and I thought it was a good idea when we overheard Kuo telling my mother about it. We grinned at each other when we thought about Metal in his new outfit and whether he would actually consent to wearing it.

Metal's first day in class sparked a bit of commotion and uneasiness among his fellow students. Kuo stroked his chin thoughtfully at the sight of this massive hulk in his mid-thirties lumbering into the room and because he was acutely aware of the physical challenges the man would have to face almost wrote him off. In a typically generous and good-natured move, Kuo decided to experiment, patiently crafting a method of instruction with Metal that he hoped would accomplish the desired results. Metal reciprocated by showing dedication and a profound desire to learn. Over time, Uncle transformed the muscle bound giant into a well-oiled machine that moved with grace and precision, resulting in the two of them becoming fast friends.

Fa and I remembered Metal shaking our hands vigorously as we left the aircraft hanger and telling us that we were welcome to stop by anytime we liked to watch him work. His work later enabled him to enjoy a modest success, and to this day, my wife and I have tried to stay in touch with him, but he moved around quite a bit. His health has declined in recent years, and he has had his share of troubles dealing drugs, but he helped me out of a couple of scrapes as a teenager, and I've always thought of him fondly. For now, my brother and I decided we liked him.

The uniforms turned out better than expected. The students were relieved because they liked Earth Mother and were afraid to say anything that might risk hurting her feelings. After taking everyone's measurements, Earth poured herself into the task. She set about cutting the various patterns for the arms, legs, torsos, and sleeves out of heavy cloth. Then she chose navy for color and paid special attention to detail, adorning each jacket with frog buttons and Mandarin collars. Even Kuo was impressed, asking her if she'd ordered them from China. Earth beamed with satisfaction, and everyone was delighted. Uncle showed Earth Mother his wide brimmed fedora with the accompanying story of the three beautiful women who made it. Ling Ling always smiled when she heard this story. I pictured three Ling Ling's in a room making it for him, turning it into the sleek article of perfection it once had been. Now that they were officially clad, the five-core group settled into a bond that was destined to last over a great many years.

Kuo was astounded at the fact that Mei cooked dinner every night, but that Harry Chen never took the family out to a restaurant, a fact my brother and I took for granted because we never knew any different. One day, he could stand it no longer and spoke to my mother in Chinese. I translated in English for Fa as we remained hidden behind the crack of our bedroom door.

"Mei, it's time your sons were around other grownup people for a change. Jimmy and I would like to take the boys out to dinner tomorrow."

My mother smiled up at him and placed her hands on his cheeks. "I'll have them ready by six," she said. Mother didn't see us jumping up and down on our bedroom floor. We knew whenever our Uncle Kuo was involved, some kind of adventure wouldn't be far behind. Good or bad, we didn't care. We were primed and ready when the time came.

Jimmy's old Volkswagen Beetle rattled up to the shop door precisely at six p.m. Mother fussed a bit with our clip-on bow ties, making sure they were straight, and gave us both a kiss.

"Now promise me you'll behave and act like young gentlemen tonight, boys," she said in a cautioning tone. We promised, elbowing our way through the front door and running out into the street with the shop bell clanging furiously behind us. Uncle Kuo reached out of his window to open the car door, and we were off.

Being a passenger with Jimmy Chow at the wheel could be an exciting or harrowing experience, depending on one's age. He liked to stay a step ahead of the New York cabbies, making sure his wheel climbed the curb first before the cabbies even started turning theirs. Fa and I looked at each other and grinned. When he reached the brink of the nerve-wracking stage, Uncle clucked his tongue.

"Come on Jimmy, this isn't Beijing. Remember, we have two youngsters on board, and I would still like the use of my legs when we get there."

"Sorry, Master Kuo," said Jimmy cheerfully lighting a cigarette.

"And we'll have none of that either," Kuo said to him sternly. Jimmy pitched it.

As daylight made a hazy retreat, we pulled up in front of a restaurant that bore my mother's maiden name, Mei Fong's. All of us piled out at once. Uncle retrieved the ticket from the valet and we walked inside, feeling important. The restaurant was warm and mostly candlelit, with a large red candle at each table. Two attendants helped us off with our coats, and the proprietor, a Japanese American woman named Jocelyn, showed us to our table. My uncle was particularly fond of Jocelyn, but he could have wished for her all he liked, and it would have done him no good because she was married to the other proprietor and executive chef of the restaurant, Arthur Fong. Mei Fong's was named for their eldest daughter. Arthur Fong had been a lethal Katana swordsman in Japan as well as a tough and shrewd businessman. The Chinese and the Japanese often expressed hatred for each other due to their various bloody conflicts, which lasted centuries. Kuo took exception to this. He respected and cherished his handful of Japanese friends, particularly Arthur and Jocelyn.

Once we had been seated, a waiter ceremoniously presented us each with our menus. He then waved the napkins off the table and onto our laps. Fa and I raised our hands to our mouths and started to giggle. Uncle gently snatched the menus out of our hands.

"I think I will order for us tonight, boys, and you can do it next time, all right?" He called the waiter back over.

It was an evening I remember to this day in spectacular detail for many reasons but mostly because the food was so incredibly delicious. We dined first on smoked duck soup, followed by a ginger scallion red snapper that was served with steaming bowls of Japanese ramen noodles on the side. When it was over, Jimmy and Uncle sat back contemplatively sipping their liqueurs.

After a period of silence, Fa and I decided to ask our Uncle a question about his art that we weren't sure was actually truth or a rumour. "Uncle," we both began, then Fa stopped short and I continued. "Uncle, we have heard that there are martial arts masters in China who can extinguish the flame of a candle from a long distance. Is this true?"

The two men smiled at each other. "And from whom did you hear such nonsense?" said my uncle, trying to suppress a smile.

"It was from a school friend, Uncle," I replied. "He said he once lived in Taiwan."

"Did he now?" said Kuo, trying to stifle a guffaw. Jimmy laughed. "Did he say it looked anything like this?"

Uncle pointed two fingers at a nearby table where a couple was enjoying an intimate moment, holding hands by candlelight. The candle on their table instantly snuffed out and they were plunged into darkness. The couple's jaws dropped. The entire restaurant suddenly went dead and everyone stopped what they were doing, including the wait staff. We looked around, and people were staring at us.

"My dear Kuo Yun San!" came a booming voice from the kitchen area in the back. Arthur Fong appeared, placing both his hands affectionately on Kuo's shoulders. "I see you have lost none of your old magic, but for pity's sake, will you stop frightening my customers?"

Uncle laughed and stood up to greet our jovial proprietor. "Arthur," said Uncle beaming with pride. "Dinner was exceptional tonight. These are my two young nephews, Paulie and Fa. Paulie is growing up to be a young man, so we are now calling him Paul."

"Hello, Paul," said Arthur Fong, enclosing his immense hand over my little paw. "Hello, Fa," he said. "I knew your uncle when he was a great martial artist in China. I see he still has a couple of tricks up his sleeve," he added with a twinkle in his eye. "Can I interest you boys in some dessert? My wife Jocelyn baked us this huge chocolate cake today." My brother and I looked pleadingly at my uncle. Uncle scratched the stubble on his chin thoughtfully.

"Shame to have it all go to waste," continued the owner, shaking his head wistfully. "Now I'll have to feed it to that big cat next door." Our pleas escalated and we started to salivate.

Kuo chuckled. "Arthur Fong you are a shameless manipulator. All right we'll each have a piece." The table cheered. "But give Jimmy a small one. He's training students tomorrow, and I want him lean and fit."

Jimmy Chow, who was thin as a rail, looked over with a pained expression. Then he lit a cigarette while imitating a cat, clawing the air and making growling noises until Fa and I roared. Jimmy continued to entertain us with jokes until it was time to leave. Kuo rose and reluctantly said goodbye to Jocelyn, kissing her lightly on the cheek. I noticed Arthur watching them from behind a window in the kitchen door. He knew Kuo was a charming rogue even into his early sixties, and he always kept one eye on Jocelyn whenever he was around. I couldn't resist one final look back inside the restaurant. People were still staring at us.

"Give Arthur my best, and thank him for a wonderful dinner," said Kuo. He tipped the valet, and we rode home past brilliantly lit skyscrapers in contented silence. Fa and I couldn't believe our luck. We had a real story in our back pockets to tell our friends.

Chapter 8

Kuo was leading a class in the park one morning when he abruptly stopped and told everyone to take a break. It was a freezing March day despite glittering sunlight. Students milled around, stamping their feet and clapping their hands to their shoulders to keep warm. Kuo paced back and forth in front of the group as usual whenever he was about to give an important talk. In later years, I realized this was done deliberately to keep the student's attention focused on him.

The time had come to show the students that Taichi, sometimes spelled Taiji, or more accurately T'ai Chi, derived from its Pinyin spelling, had teeth and could be used effectively for self defence. T'ai Chi is in fact a martial arts training exercise that the Chinese turned into a regimen for health. The idea of using slow movement from a martial perspective is to practice unifying all parts of the body. With proper training, a Taichi fighter can harness the forces of nature against an opponent yet appear relaxed as if nothing was happening.

Uncle was determined to prove to his students on this day that Taichi was not just an exercise for the elderly. He grabbed Fire gently by the forearm and brought the pale redhead out in front of the ranks to face the class. He then motioned one of his senior students to stand several hundred feet back. Sally Waterman, Fire's girlfriend, pressed forward between the curious students and onlookers to get a better view. Fire and Uncle Kuo seemed to approach each other warily like a couple of big cats, intertwining and touching forearms in an exercise known as Push Hands; a type of awareness and sensitivity training. The crowd was startled by a noise resembling a loud pop and Fire with his shock of red hair was propelled backwards with such violent speed into the arms of Kuo's awaiting assistant that they both almost fell over. The audience reaction was mixed. Some of the students were stunned, and some of them started laughing.

Then everyone applauded. Sally was more than a little relieved to see that her boyfriend was all right as she knew Kuo could be rough on his students. She clapped along with everyone else and smiled. Kuo beamed back at her and ushered Fire back into the crowd.

The odd thing was it looked as if Uncle Kuo had expended no energy whatsoever except for a slight turning and shifting of the hips. Next he crooked his index finger at Sally, beckoning her to step out in front of the group. Now he really had everyone's attention. Kuo hid a smile, watching his audience stare in rapt silence at the frail, attractive young girl who seemed about to meet her fate.

"Sally is very angry at me for looking at another woman and has decided to punch me hard in the face," Kuo announced to some general laughter among the growing gallery of onlookers.

Sally shot him back a wry smile. Kuo nodded at her and she sent him a high-speed right hand punch about eye level. Kuo disappeared like smoke. As Sally's fist hurled into the void, Uncle suddenly reappeared from behind, tapping her on the shoulder. Kuo thought the whole thing hilarious, but his students, not to mention the onlookers, had never seen anything like it before. Some were uncomfortable and even a little frightened. "Taichi is an illusion!" thundered Uncle. "But..." He pointed to his head, ". . . you must always know what your enemy is thinking."

Applause resumed among the disoriented crowd. Some students in attendance felt Kuo proved his point and that he probably shouldn't reveal any more. Little did they know he was just getting started. Kuo went on to demonstrate the capabilities of Taichi's various weapons with the senior students: the straight sword, broadsword, halberd, and spear. He then demonstrated he couldn't be moved from one spot, even while being pushed by four strong men and included an amazing display in which he fought off several attackers at once. Students attending that day said they had never seen such a high level of mastery in martial art before or since.

Subsequent to these events, Fa and I began to notice uncle becoming a familiar presence in our Chinatown dry goods store, not because, as he claimed, it was the only place in town that he could shop for exotic ingredients such as dried baby whitefish or marinated oxtail, nor because of the many other popularly sought after items like Chinese beer, almond butter cookies, and Taiwanese cigarettes. None of these things, it seemed, were as intoxicating to my uncle as the most recent addition to the store, a new shop girl and friend of my mother's, known only by her former married name, Mrs. Liang.

As a welcome treat, my mother occasionally kept a simmering pot of Kimchee on a small portable stove. The powerful aroma of marinated cabbage saturated the store for most of the afternoon, and customers were allowed to sample a modest amount by ladling chunks of cabbage from the potent brew into small earthenware bowls. Kuo and Mrs. Liang could often be seen sipping Kimchee broth and chatting cosily together in a corner whenever she was afforded a break. We also noticed that Uncle's bachelorhood had become a favourite object of scrutiny at family gatherings. Uncle usually shrugged off the family prying with a good-natured laugh, telling us that he enjoyed his bachelor lifestyle and that he preferred being left to his own devices. Lately, however, he remained mysteriously quiet at the table, especially when that subject was brought up.

My brother and I were not at all fascinated by Mrs. Liang. We didn't take to her right off the way our uncle did. She peered at us through a pair of gold-rimmed spectacles then wandered off muttering something incoherent under her breath. Fa screwed up his face and stuck out his tongue at her as soon as her back was turned, which always made me laugh, but if mother or another grownup were present, I pretended to admonish him for it.

Mrs. Liang came from a coastal region in China known as Fujian. Harry Chen called people that came from this region "container people," alluding to the unfortunate and sometimes disastrous practice of Chinese families smuggling themselves into other countries by means of shipping containers. Some of them made it, but many died of suffocation and dehydration. Human remains were sometimes discovered trying to claw their way out.

Mrs. Liang, however, came over with her family by freighter the same way Uncle Kuo had. The family immediately found work in a textile factory, sleeping on the factory floors at night, hidden with the help of employees until they could obtain citizenship papers. My mother, who bought cloth wholesale to make her embroidered napkins and table coverings, met Mrs. Liang where she worked. Over several cups of coffee the two became fast friends. Mother wasted no time in offering Mrs. Liang a job at the store, promising her better wages and working conditions.

Mrs. Liang showed up for work that same week, immediately assuming her lofty perch on a wooden stool behind the sales counter. From her makeshift crow's nest, she supervised store activities, organizing everyone's comings and goings from the mix of servants, purveyors, and customers until she was satisfied that all were in their proper place, doing what they were supposed to be doing. Predictably, Mother's long-term clients chafed at the unwelcome and slightly bossy intrusion but gradually learned to put up with it, if only because they knew Mother valued Mrs. Liang and felt she was being a help.

No matter how tired Harry Chen was from toiling eleven hours a day as branch manager of a Chinatown bank, he never seemed to grow weary of needling Uncle about his newfound relationship. It seemed he had discovered a never-ending source of amusement.

"So, Uncle," he began, his face melting into a huge grin. "How are you and Mrs. uh... what's-her-name..."

"Liang," Uncle finished.

"Yes, that's it, Mrs. Liang... getting along?"

"She is a very kind and wise woman," Kuo usually answered, then changed the subject.

My stepfather laughingly confided to my mother that they were the oddest looking pair he he'd ever seen. My mother, on the other hand, made it look as if she was encouraging the unlikely romance without revealing whether she thought they were right for each other. Mei had always been a great believer in everything "happening for a reason." Mrs. Liang was a widow and Kuo a bachelor. What could be more natural than to make some effort to unite them?

Mother made suggestive little touches like bringing a small vase of wildflowers over to a table where Kuo and Mrs. Liang would be sitting. Sometimes she shooed Fa and I away if she thought they might be sharing an intimate moment. Once, when Fa was patrolling the storerooms for candy bars, he caught them in a private embrace. This was a troubling new wrinkle, and my brother and I were decidedly unhappy about it. Besides being a dearly venerated uncle, Kuo was also our friend. Both of us hated the evil Mrs. Liang, and felt that she might try to change him in some way, or worse, turn him against us.

Kuo, for his part, was falling hard. He wooed his new girlfriend away from her duties at the dry goods store and made her his receptionist. Then he offered her a raise, subsidized out of his own pocket. In that whole time, Mrs. Liang never changed her demeanour towards us. The one exception was my mother, whom she always treated nicely and with respect.

In some ways, it was a relief that Mrs. Liang was leaving. My brother and I were finally rid of her. Our celebration was short-lived, however, when we learned that she would be replacing Ling Ling at the T'ai Chi School's reception area. Ling Ling had been working part-time as a receptionist and personal assistant to my uncle, who now seemed to be replacing her with no more thought than acquiring a new toothbrush. She was also pretty, with a sunny disposition and had all the customers eating out of her hand. How I looked forward to seeing her every time we paid a visit to the studio, but no more. Now the lovely smile that brightened my day would be replaced by a narrow frown, and I was far from the only one displeased. Jimmy Chow was incensed.

"Why this woman, Kuo? Why does she make a face like a sour prune? And God, those *glasses!*" He pressed both hands to his face and pushed them upwards through his hair in exasperation.

Kuo put his arm around Jimmy's shoulders and took him out for a few beers.

When they returned, Jimmy seemed to be in good spirits and back to his old self. Kuo had won him over as usual. Where Kuo's students were concerned, however, this wasn't going to be so easy.

Chapter 9

The school had been buzzing with excitement for the past two months. My uncle had decided to enter five of his top students in a regional T'ai Chi tournament. In stark contrast to these events, he simultaneously decided to end his long bachelorhood and tie the knot. Few people came to the small reception, which was not held at our home as mother had hoped. Mrs. Liang, prim and proper as usual, was well turned out for the occasion which most of our family attended. I remember there was only one thing that struck us as a bit peculiar. Mrs. Liang had expressed no desire to change her married name and would henceforth always be referred to as Mrs. Liang, a fact my uncle merely accepted without protest. My mother complimented her on her wedding dress and told her she looked pretty. In a way, she did.

The week was brimming with milestones. Kuo, without a word to either of us, made the decision to enter Fa and myself into the sword routine competition. We had each made progress since our days spent practicing on the upstairs porch under his watchful eye. We received coaching privately after school and often stopped by to watch the students. Now he was anxious for us to experience the work that went into getting our teammates and us ready for a competition.

"That bastard Xiao Feng is going to be there from the Beijing Wushu Team," Kuo muttered in a low tone, biting his fingernails. He hissed out the name, "Sheeeeow Fung. He's going to be one of the judges."

Xiao Feng, it was said, drilled students until they succumbed to nervous exhaustion. "I want you two boys to polish up your Chen sword routines and do your best. Understand?" Fa and I nodded in unison as we usually did when a figure of authority was speaking to us.

Five major styles of T'ai Chi are practiced throughout the world. Of these, the Chen style, is said to be the oldest and to retain more of the traditional characteristics. It is also slightly more physical looking, making it popular with audiences.

The core group, nicknamed Earth, Fire, Water, Metal, and Wood, was selected to represent the school as well as Ling Ling and some other senior students. Ling Ling went pale, and her hands turned to ice when she heard she would be performing for the ruthless teacher, Xiao Feng, a long-time member of the Communist Party and an ill-tempered perfectionist. As for the rest of the students, who were oblivious, this was business as usual; another one of Master Kuo's attempts to broaden their horizons. Most were exhilarated to show off what they'd learned and greeted the news enthusiastically.

Sensing Ling Ling's nervousness, Kuo took her quietly aside. He sat down with her and massaged her fingers.

"Your hands are freezing," he said. "And you're losing your concentration." Then he put his arm around her shoulder in a fatherly gesture. "Let me worry about judges," he said. She started in, but he put a finger up to his lips. "And not a word to the students either, O.K.?" he asked, giving her a meaningful look.

"I don't want you or the students to worry about these things," he said. "Leave these matters to me." The distraught Ling Ling put her head on Kuo's shoulder and felt comfort there as we all had from time to time.

Earth Mother excitedly told everyone she planned to sew together a large banner with Kuo Yun San T'ai Chi School emblazoned on the front, but Mrs. Liang for some reason turned down the idea. A veritable uproar ensued that put Mrs. Liang in the middle of some heated protests by the students. Earth Mother, though visibly disappointed, took the news good-naturedly, but for the students, it was another matter. A personal line had been drawn in the sand.

My uncle discreetly removed the unpopular Mrs. Liang from her post, and thereafter her duties consisted of light typing and occasional filing in the back office. Though my uncle respected and dearly loved his new wife, he knew she could be difficult and often saw retreat as the best way out of delicate situations. My brother and I were asked to fill in, greeting students and taking names on rosters. We were also asked to keep track of some of the accounts. I was happy. This had become my first real job, and best of all, though Uncle was never particularly generous, we were getting paid.

Amidst the heady activity of those summer months, no one seemed a bit concerned that Fa and I were shedding our adolescence and growing into manhood. For the first time, I noticed some facial hair on my upper lip and became irritable over insignificant things. Worst of all, my voice was changing. Fa had problems of his own. He was struggling with nocturnal emissions and beginning to notice women, women whose glances told us, in no uncertain terms, that we wouldn't be able to coast through life on our looks.

What with schoolwork, manning the reception desk, and practicing for the tournament, there was thankfully little time to dwell on any of these matters. Kuo kept us busy as beavers. In fact, we were kept so busy that there was scarcely time to address a new and troublesome figure that loomed large in Fa's life at about that time. He was a school bully, someone who'd only recently turned his attentions to the hapless target my little brother had become. I offered my services to get rid of him, but Fa, mortified even by the suggestion, refused.

Uncle Kuo got wind of the problem through our stepfather, Harry Chen, whom Fa eventually confided to in tears. The bully had already challenged my brother to a fight in the school courtyard after last period class. "...and you better not run like a scared little baby, or I'll really let you have it" were his last words.

When Kuo learned that Fa's enemy was a large muscular chap who played for the school football team, he invited us both over to his apartment in Queens. Uncle sent me off around the corner to get some cigarettes and a newspaper then sat Fa down at his modest dining room table. Kuo took the kettle off a small stove in the corner of the room, poured some water into it, and lit the burner. After he had replaced the kettle on the stove, he asked Fa if he would like some tea. My little brother shook his head dismally, already thinking of the humiliation he would soon have to face from his fellow classmates. Uncle pulled up a chair and sat looking out the window.

"Have I ever told you the story of the Samurai and the man who made tea?" he asked. Fa shook his head again, eyes glued to the floor. Uncle ignored him and continued. "Once a lowly peasant was pushing a cart filled with pig manure around a local village, trying to sell it for fertilizer. Just as he came around the corner with the wheelbarrow, a Samurai walked out of a shop and stepped right in front of him. Too late to stop, the man ran straight into the Samurai, spilling pig manure all over him. Everyone who saw it started laughing. The Samurai was very angry. He challenged the peasant to a duel and told the peasant to meet him at dawn the next morning in the town square. The peasant was very frightened because Samurai were expert swordsmen and always fought to the death as part of their code of honour.

"He looked for the wisest man in the village to ask for advice. When the peasant found the man he was looking for, the man was at home, making tea, and invited the peasant inside. The peasant was restless because the man said nothing but continued preparing the tea in a very slow manner. Finally, the peasant could stand it no longer and broke down, telling the man what had happened to him. The man said, 'My son, you see how I am making this tea? Just make tea.'

"The peasant didn't understand the old man's advice until he woke up the next morning. He slowly got out of bed, did his meditation, and said a prayer. Then he got dressed, put on his armour, strapped on a sword and shield, and went out to face the Samurai. When the Samurai saw the peasant coming towards him ready to fight, he turned and went his way."

"That's a nice story, Uncle," said Fa, but he was not to be so easily consoled.

When I returned we chatted awhile until it was time to leave. Fa decided to have a cup of Uncle's tea after all.

That very next day, the dreaded bell sounded for third period. Fa, with the courage of a Christian holding four aces, stepped out on the tarmac to face the bully down.

Chapter 10

The effect of the school's rear lot, with its two-story high wire fences, gave one the impression of being in a prison yard. The kids, hearing that there was going to be a fight, stormed out of the school and began to gather around, hoping to see some blood.

The bully had been laughing and joking with some of his friends in a corner, but when he caught sight of Fa, he walked up to him as though trying to block his path. Fa dropped his book bag and got into a defensive Shaolin posture my uncle had taught him. He held his right hand flat out in front of him and guarded his chest with the left. Then his eyes narrowed and he stared over his palm like someone sighting down the barrel of a gun. He stood there quiet and motionless. A smile crept over the bully's face.

"I heard your uncle was some kind of famous fighter in China, pinhead," the bully called out. "Is that true?"

"That's none of your business," Fa shot back defiantly. "Besides, it's just the two of us here. What are you waiting for?"

The huge boy folded his arms and stared at Fa for a while. Then an astonishing thing happened. Uncle Kuo's tale turned into a self-fulfilling prophecy as my little brother watched his enemy suddenly laugh and then amble away with his arms around his buddies.

Fa's friends crowded around him and cheered, patting him vigorously on the back. Glad that I didn't have to step in and completely wreck an already lousy school day, I applauded Fa myself and offered to take him to the soda fountain for a milkshake. He declined and suggested that we meet that evening at the studio to train for a while before going home. I happily accepted his offer. I was proud of my little brother that day; he had shown amazing spirit. Best of all, Ling Ling had switched her schedule at my uncle's studio. She had been working most evenings and there was a good chance I would get to see her.

As an odd footnote to all this, I brought up the incident of the bully to Fa many years later when we were grown men in our thirties. It seemed that he and the bully had made up over the years but it was their high school sweethearts who kept in touch, forming a lasting relationship.

Straight out of the frying pan into the fire, our lives would soon be consumed by the T'ai Chi tournament, due to take place a scant three weeks later. When the day finally arrived, I could safely say that we were all nervous wrecks, except for Ling Ling, who seemed the picture of calm. It was a distorted picture. Beneath the serene exterior of a young woman sitting in the bleachers of an indoor auditorium, mindfully polishing her sword, was a sweaty mess of a girl who felt as if she could throw up any minute. She had gotten there hours ahead of us, which might have been a tip off as to her impaired mental state, but thankfully wasn't. No one was the wiser, of course, except for my Uncle Kuo. After sending us off to change into our uniforms and get ready, he scooted down on the bench close to Ling Ling, addressing her by her proper name.

"Did you get some sleep last night, Ba Ling?" he asked.

"I slept very well, thank you," she replied icily.

"If you would feel more comfortable," he began, "I could put you in a little ahead of...."

"I feel just fine," she interrupted, arching her perfect eyebrows. "I want to go on exactly as planned."

"All right then, as you say."

My uncle, who hadn't slept all that well the night before, sighed exhaustedly. Some families began to arrive, making their slow procession through the bleachers. They were followed sometime later by the auditorium staff, teachers, and finally the judges. Xiao Feng, the great wushu teacher, made his entrance last. Surrounded by his entourage, he smiled broadly for a few pictures and shook hands with the promoters. Kuo, seizing the opportunity to get it over with, strode up to him and extended his hand.

"So *you* are here!" Xiao Feng sputtered in amazement, raising one eyebrow. "I thought I saw your name on the program, but I couldn't believe it. We thought we'd seen your backside forever the day you left the mainland."

He spoke to my uncle in Cantonese, but Kuo replied in English. "It's a great honour to meet with you once again, Dr. Feng. I can see the years have been kind."

"As they have to you," Xiao Feng said in his haltingly exaggerated English. "I see you have a school now and American students. Good." Then Feng switched back to Cantonese and smiled as he left my uncle with a few parting words of encouragement. "Enjoy your funeral," he said. "And good luck, you are going to need it."

My uncle smiled back at him, bowed, and temporarily left the panel to speak to my brother and I. "Who were you talking to just then? Is that Xiao Feng?" I asked.

"No one," replied Uncle. "You two are up first after the Chinatown Kung Fu School, so get yourselves ready."

Shortly after Xiao Feng was seated, the Beijing wushu students arrived in their bright yellow satin uniforms with all the fanfare of a circus troop. They broke off into somersaults, stretching, jumping, and acrobatically windmilling themselves across the makeshift stages. This was their way of psyching out the competition, and it often had its desired effect.

"Just look at them," demurred Earth Mother. Kuo and Fire gave each other a meaningful look. Then Kuo walked away with a sneer, muttering something under his breath that was clear even if you couldn't understand it.

Our school's modest program went roughly like this: Fa and I would go on first together, shadowing each other and giving the audience two angles from which to observe our straight sword routine. Uncle was adamant that we perform exactly as he had instructed us without deviating or trying to put our own style into it. Next would be Fire and Sally Waterman, paired off in the broadsword category. Then Metal would give a shirtless demonstration of the twin golden melon hammers to lights and heavy rock music. The twin hammers were two huge gothic-like antique weapons, requiring great strength to manipulate. They had been used during the Chinese Warring of the States period for smashing armour or skulls, which ever came first. Wood and Earth Mother would demonstrate push hands, and Ling Ling would perform her double straight sword routine and demonstrate some martial arts applications of T'ai Chi Chuan at the end of the program.

None of those latter events would occur. Our involvement in the tournament was cut short out of concern for Ling Ling who had, defying my uncle's advice, starved herself for days and slept only a few hours a night while training. The girl suddenly went pale and passed out cold during her double straight sword routine which was known for pushing the body to its limits. Her breathing stopped momentarily, and because I happened to be close at hand, I gave her mouth-to-mouth resuscitation the way we had been taught in school. I couldn't help wondering about the ironies of life as I bent over her, pumping her chest and blowing short bursts of air into her mouth. If she was to regain consciousness at that moment, what was she to think?

She started to come around slowly. I could have kissed her right there but resorted to smoothing back her hair and dabbing her sweaty forehead with a damp cloth while she moaned in my arms. An ambulance was called and Ling Ling was taken away on a stretcher, still very weak.

"I'm really sorry, but our school is going to have to withdraw from the tournament for the rest of the day," said my uncle sadly, addressing the panel of judges. He knew it would mean certain forfeiture and even possible expulsion from future tournaments. Xiao Feng smirked at his neighbour and then stood up.

"It seems avoiding responsibility has become a habit for you," he sneered at Kuo. "Is it possible that the great Kuo Yun San is avoiding the larger issue here which is the fact that his students are both disobedient and ill-prepared? Perhaps he should not have wasted our time in the first place."

"It is true that my students are American, that they have a long way to go and a lot to learn. It is also true that they have not had the benefit of being exposed to much Chinese culture or tradition. But I think you'll agree they mostly did well today and are deserving of our respect and support."

Mrs. Liang, who had been within earshot of the conversation, jumped in to everyone's surprise. "Master Xiao Feng," she said, addressing him loudly. "Do you not remember my first cousin General Chang Hue?"

Xiao Feng's jaw dropped as if the breath had been knocked out of him. This was a name that struck terror into the hearts of many a Communist leader made to undergo long dreadful purges and months of imprisonment at the general's hands.

"Are...are you..." he stammered wide-eyed.

"I am Mrs. Liang," she said sternly, "And master Kuo is my husband. I think that both he and his students were very brave taking time to come here and demonstrate for you today not knowing what challenges they would have to face. I knew you as a soldier during the period of the Long March when I was a little girl, and no one thought of you as a great fighter then. And here you are, disrespecting my husband."

Xiao Feng turned beet red and resumed his seat.

"If the distinguished panel will please excuse us," Kuo interjected, "Miss Ba Ling is a close and dear friend of ours, and we will soon be leaving for the hospital to attend to her at this time. We are grateful for the honour and opportunity you have afforded us to be here today, but we must leave now.

Xiao Feng was the first to stand and extend his hand to Uncle Kuo. "It's been a long time since anyone has talked to me like that," he said, reverting to his favourite Cantonese language which he felt was indicative of a superior education. "You're right, your students did quite well today, and you should be proud of them."

Then he pulled Kuo in close and whispered to him, "The young girl, Ba Ling, is good. She has obviously benefited from your instruction, and your two nephews are showing promise."

Kuo thanked him. Then after shaking hands with everyone and saying a final farewell, he took his wife by the arm and escorted her out of the building where Jimmy Chow was waiting to take them to the hospital. Fire, my brother and I, and several students were in hot pursuit behind them in Fire's V.W. microbus, pedal to the floor.

Chapter 11

Kuo scolded his new wife. "Did you not think I had the situation under control?" he asked her through pursed lips. "In future, please...I know you mean well." Then after a while, he softened and stroked a strand of hair that fell across her cheek.

When we were finally allowed to visit the hospital room, we found Ling Ling waving and giving us a weak smile behind an oxygen tent. She was fine. They kept her overnight for observation and released her the next morning. Kuo mouthed the words. "Xiao Feng thinks you're great!" and gave her a big two thumbs up which she returned with a huge grin.

Looking back on that fateful day, I would still have been proud to be counted alongside my uncle's American students. We did pretty well. And the best or worst news of all, though I played it down at every opportunity, was that my fellow students were hailing me as the hero who saved Ba Ling.

Ba Ling for her part was thoroughly humiliated by entire episode and refused to discuss it with anyone. She privately thanked me for my services as paramedic and then made me swear not to mention the incident to a soul outside of our school acquaintances.

I told her someday I might tell my grandchildren, and I ended up doing just that, but for now I swore I wouldn't mention anything to anyone. It's one of a select group of promises I've managed to keep throughout my life. Truth be told, all the attention was becoming somewhat of a humiliation fest for me as well, and I was relieved when the subject was finally dropped.

Kuo decided to throw a small mixer for his students at Jimmy Chow's loft in New Jersey. He was desperate to reward them all for rising to the occasion, and he hoped he'd be able to turn the past days events into a happy memory.

Not surprisingly, the little party they cooked up was a howling success. Jimmy Chow's tiny loft was packed to the rafters with revellers deep into the wee hours. Kuo walked around to each of the students, complimenting them on how well they did and making suggestions about what areas he felt they needed to work on. Fa and I were put in charge of serving refreshments but sternly prohibited from imbibing any alcohol ourselves. That evening everyone gathered around Jimmy's rabbit eared T.V. set to watch President Johnson give his State of the Union Address.

"He is a man with large ears. He must be very wise," said Kuo.

Everyone laughed. Around that time Fa and I managed to sneak out to the fire escape with a couple of bottles of beer and two cigarettes stolen from one of Jimmy's heavily lacquered cigarette cases. Fa fumbled with the matches and was just about to give us a successful light when we heard a sliding door open over our heads. I quickly blew out the match and motioned Fa not to make a sound. At first what we heard was muffled, like two people speaking very far away in a foreign tongue. But as we continued eavesdropping, we recognized the voices as coming from Kuo and Ling Ling. They were speaking in Mandarin.

"You know.... I never told you what your favourite Communist teacher said to me about you."

"What?" asked Ling Ling sounding a little tipsy.

Kuo paused for effect and we could hear sounds of him lighting his pipe. "Well..." he began, taking his time between puffs, "It's like this..."

"Oh come on, tell me," pleaded Ling Ling.

"That rude bastard, who calls himself a teacher, told me he thought you were pretty good," Kuo said finally.

"Really?" Ling Ling gushed. "Are you being serious?"

It was in the middle of Uncle's next sentence that Fa dropped the matches. They landed with a clatter on the stairwell. Both of us held our breath and bit our lips.

"Is anyone down there?" called my uncle. The voice was met with as much silence as we could muster.

"Must be one of Jimmy's cats," murmured Ling Ling. After a while we heard the sliding glass door open again and they were back inside. Gasping a collective sigh of relief, we popped open the beer bottles but after a couple of sips threw them away and never did get to smoke our cigarettes.

As we started to go back inside, Uncle's two giant hands appeared eerily out of the darkness, landing on the backs of on our shoulders. We jumped about a foot. "Boys, you did me proud at the tournament. Fa, you have learned everything I taught you well, and Paulie, you are beginning to develop good technique." Then he winked, "Just don't try to hide anything from me, all right?"

As if we could, I thought to myself, looking up at the stars. Re-entering Jimmy Chow's loft, we found the students crowded around in a circle under a haze of cigarette smoke.

They motioned us to join them. Jimmy poured cups of strong tea some Burmese friends had left him and we all sat down. Some of the students, feeling the full weight of the evening's libations, became increasingly self-critical. Those who had been showered with praise earlier now felt as if it were incumbent upon them to show an exaggerated sense of humility, whether for Uncle's benefit or not, we were uncertain.

Metal admitted that some of his routine with the giant twin melon hammers had been sloppy and felt dissatisfied about the choice of music.

Fire and Sally complained that they didn't feel like they were in synch during the broadsword routine and Earth Mother admonished Wood for too much roughhousing during the ensuing push hands demonstration. I then pitched in and accused Fa of not paying attention during the Chen sword routine, and he in turn blamed me for going too fast.

The scene turned into a full out bickering match. Kuo looked at Jimmy who shook his head. Ling Ling, who had been nursing a bottle of rice wine most of the evening, stared at Jimmy's Oriental rug dejectedly, tears of disappointment welling up in her eyes. The entire convivial mood was beginning to deteriorate. Earth Mother put a stop to it by raising her beer bottle.

"Now listen all of you," she said. "I happen to know something that most of you don't." The room fell silent and all eyes focused in her direction. "Master Kuo was kind enough to share some information with me about the tournament he wanted kept secret so we wouldn't get all distracted and nervous and mess things up. As it so happens, one of the judges was a famous teacher from Beijing. Master said he once chaired the Chinese International Martial Arts Committee and that he'd won many awards; isn't that so, Master Kuo?"

Kuo, who was caught off guard, could only nod silently while the students stared at each other in amazement.

"And the clincher," she went on, relishing the moment of rapt attention, "was that he said we had made a terrific effort and that Master should be proud of us." You could have heard a pin drop. Kuo kept nodding in agreement. "So now I would like to propose a toast to everyone at this wonderful school who did their best. Let's really show 'em what we can do next time!" Then she hollered "Gan Bei!" which meant "Cheers," or "Drain the cup," in Chinese. Everyone yelled "Gan Bei!" and the laughter and jovial tenure of the evening returned in full force.

"When were you planning to tell the rest of us about this, Master Kuo?" Sally teased. But as Kuo was about to answer, the heavy cigarette smoke in the room became infused with a sweeter earthier type of smell. Those who were unaware kept on chatting away, but to Uncle, who'd pulled many a befuddled friend from hash dens in Hong Kong and to Jimmy Chow who'd worked a police beat on the mean streets of Shanghai, the shared recognition was instantaneous.

Both identified the odour as cannabis mixed with hashish. Uncle and Jimmy discreetly excused themselves, and then soon afterward we heard familiar footsteps clattering down the stairwell in the distance and knew they had gone to investigate.

Chapter 12

Mrs. Liang, who had been conspicuously absent from the proceedings, now showed up late, bottle of wine in hand. She proceeded to unscrew the cap and sit cross legged on the floor next to Ling Ling, by now fatally drunk to the point of being despondent. They conversed in Mandarin; sharing, as near as I could make out, their mutually disparaging feelings about men. Mrs. Liang poured two glasses of wine for her and Ling Ling then looked around the room. "Where's my husband?" she asked.

Reaching the bottom of the stairwell, Uncle and Jimmy happened upon a couple of longhaired blond figures standing in the hallway. Peace signs were sewn into the backs of their denim jackets, which a year earlier my uncle mistook for a crude version of the Yin Yang symbol. He bowed his head in recognition to its owners until Jimmy took him aside and filled him in as to what they meant. After that incident, Jimmy made himself responsible for bringing Kuo up to speed as comprehensively as he could on the whole "flower power" movement. It was a labour of love that yielded mixed results.

The shorter of the two individuals in the hallway produced an ornate looking pipe from which a thin layer of smoke curled toward the ceiling.

"Excuse me, ladies," said Kuo, making his trademark misidentification.

The smile on Jimmy's face drained away to recognition as the shorter of the two men turned to face them, sporting a week old growth of facial stubble.

"Ladies?" the smaller man exclaimed incredulously. "Did y' hear that Chas?" He turned to his large brute of a friend who said nothing. Then after a pause he asked, "You guys want a toke?"

Kuo ignored the question and continued. "I have some students here that I don't want to be associated with what you're doing. Please go somewhere else because we can smell it upstairs."

"Aaaw, what a nice story," said the shorter man, speaking in a heavy Bronx accent through his teeth as he held in another hit. "Did ya heah that? Seems thuh pruffessuh heah don't want us corruptin' his students. He thinks we might be a bad influence or somethin' like dat, ain't that right proffessuh?" He walked up toward my uncle until they were inches apart and started poking him threateningly in the chest. "Well this is a free country," he went on. "So why don't you go back to gook land where you came from and tell your friends we don't take orders from chinks?" His imposing looking friend stood by silently, Jimmy thought menacingly, without turning around.

"C'mon guys," said Jimmy, trying his best to be diplomatic, "You know what you're doing is illegal..." Kuo was about to grab the man's finger when a voice came from over his shoulder.

"Everything all right down here, Master Kuo?" The two men fled in a hurry when they saw Metal's enormous frame lumbering down the stairwell, but concern lingered on Jimmy's face.

"I know I've seen those two somewhere before," he muttered thoughtfully within earshot of Kuo.

"We are fine," replied Kuo suddenly brightening. "I think I hear my wife upstairs."

The glow returned to my uncle's cheeks as they headed back up the stairs and he rubbed his hands together. "Let us forget about this," he chirped. "I believe my wife has brought a real treat for us tonight, a very special bottle of Korean rice wine that I...." But the sentence trailed off and his face fell when he re-entered the living room and found his wife next to Ling Ling. An empty bottle lay on its side, and two plastic cups sat between them.

"Weeeeell, where have you two been?" slurred Ling Ling, rising unsteadily to her feet and weaving towards Uncle Kuo with the empty bottle in her hand. "I thought we were going to have to call out the National Guard"

Mrs. Liang gave her husband a sidelong glance. Kuo gripped his young protégé by the arm and took her aside. Whispering sternly in her ear he said, "Jimmy is going to drive you home. You're drunk and my senior student. You are not going to make me lose face in front of everyone here tonight, do you understand?"

Ling Ling nodded and started to run her hand through the back of his gray hair but he waved it aside and signalled for Jimmy to take her to the car. My heart sank when I saw Ling Ling reach out to caress my uncle's hair. I could only imagine how nice her hand would feel on the back of my neck. It was at moments like this when I found myself fighting to retain my composure around her, only this time I realized that she wasn't acting quite herself. Jimmy threw a coat around her shoulders and escorted her downstairs to his car.

"It's time for you boys to be getting back too, before your mother decides to skin me alive," said Kuo matter-of-factly. We both began to raise our voices in protest, but Uncle put up a hand to silence us. "You boys were a big help tonight. I want to congratulate you on an excellent job," he said. This was accompanied by some thankful applause and lots of smiles. "I'm glad you both had a good time, and we enjoyed having you, but now it's getting late."

Then he leaned out one of the upstairs windows and gave a loud whistle to Jimmy as he was ushering Ling Ling into the car. "Hold on, Jim," he cried out. "We have two more passengers for you!" Jimmy shot back the O.K. sign, and my brother and I said our goodbyes.

Uncle gave us a big hug, keeping his arms around us for a good long time. "I'm so proud of the two of you," he said. "Now go! And tell Mei we shall all be having dinner very soon." His eyes narrowed to make sure we got the message; we promised, nearly falling as we chased each other down the stairs.

When we reached the car, I was surprised to find Ling Ling sitting in the back seat. "In case I throw up," she said, making a concerted effort to tease Jimmy by putting one hand over her mouth and making throw up noises. Fa and I cackled with laughter, but I was the one sitting next to her. She put her hand on mine and I froze for a minute, then made an effort not to melt into the seat. "Paulie, I hope you and your brother had a good time tonight," she said giving me a liquidly, lip-gloss smile. "I'm afraid your uncle's mad at me." She added with a pout, then proceeded to lay her head on my shoulder and fall asleep.

Who cares about him? I thought. I was busy enjoying the weight of her head on my shoulder and drinking in her perfume. I came to the conclusion that night that only beautiful women like Ling Ling possessed the type of scent, which had the power to annihilate men indiscriminately.

Fa looked over at us and giggled, but I was determined not to move a muscle until we reached our destination, even if my entire body went numb. It seemed like only a few minutes passed before Jimmy screeched to a halt in front of our store to let us off. I leaned in to give Ling Ling a farewell kiss, but she turned her head at the last minute, and I slipped on her cheek, tasting a mouthful of wet hair. After this she passed out cold, and I was just about getting ready to try again when Jimmy threw me a warning glance. "We are going," he said briskly. Then he rolled up the window and sped off into the rainy night, leaving me standing alone in a wet street with a few neon reflections for company.

"C'mon!" yelled Fa.

Chapter 13

By the time Jimmy got back to his loft, the party was breaking up, and he offered to take another carload. Everyone rose to shake hands, but Earth Mother, it seemed, had one final hurrah left in her. Having polished off a respectable number of beer bottles with Chinese labels on them, not to mention several cups of sake, she was determined to send everyone off with a farewell speech.

Earth Mother raised another recently emptied beer bottle, and turning to Kuo's wife, she said, "We've neglected to thank a very important person tonight." Everyone looked puzzled. "Something happened at that tournament many of you don't know about. Mrs. Liang stuck up for us when that Chinese judge got all hostile because we had to leave on account of Ling Ling." She smiled at Mrs. Liang, continuing in her broad Maine accent, "Well I was there. She got pretty doggone mad, let me tell ya, an' I never saw anyone back off so fast as that judge." Kuo placed his forehead in his palms, and everyone chuckled. Then he put his arm around his wife, kissed her apologetically, and joined in the good-natured laughter. Suddenly everyone raised their glasses and cheered Mrs. Liang.

The ice between my uncle's new wife and the students had thawed somewhat, but no one could say how long it would hold. I chalked up another night to remember, but Fa wasn't so pleased and felt that we had for the most part been treated like servants. "Leave it to our favourite uncle to make use of us," he muttered resentfully. His memory of that night and mine were universes apart. He was still a kid, while I was becoming a man.

Some of the students mocked those who were being chauffeured home as being too privileged and soft. Many threatened to walk or leave their cars and take the subway instead. This was all Kuo needed. Against the pleas of his wife whom he eventually sent home with Jimmy, Kuo stalked off toward the subway with several students in tow.

"Walking is the cure for too much alcohol and rich food," he lectured. His students laughed and kept pace with him, fuelled by each other's hubris and happy to be alive.

From the early hours of the morning on, particularly in the 1960's, a New York subway could be a lonely place, home to some of the fiercest individuals ever encountered even by the standards of preceding generations. There were fewer police patrols and no vigilante groups such as the Guardian Angels around for protection, so keeping your wits about you was standard practice.

From the perspective of hoodlums, pickpockets or muggers, Kuo and his band of young students must have seemed like easy targets. It wasn't difficult to understand how an old Chinese man, though tall and fit, surrounded by some fresh faced college kids, looked as if he wouldn't present much of a problem to anyone, let alone seasoned veterans.

That evening, Kuo was flanked by two of his most experienced Chinese students, along with Fire, Wood and Sally, who'd each been studying T'ai Chi in applied combat for more than three years. Each was trained to handle multiple attackers which gave them the combined potency of a small army even while seeming to appear vulnerable.

Kuo, as usual, had been entertaining everyone with his jokes, when five menacing individuals appeared out of nowhere.

Fire was the only one to notice that Uncle seemed more pale and fragile than usual standing behind the small group on the platform. He was aware of the fact my uncle once served as bodyguard to foreign dignitaries, most notably Madame Chiang Kai Shek. Tonight, however, the normally tall and robust sixty-year-old figure looked as if he had been reduced in size. Fire instinctually felt his master might need protection and began to draw closer to him. The five men seemed to walk right out of the walls and from behind the massive support beams.

Kuo recognized the two standing in front as the ones he and Jimmy had encountered during the party. He tried humour, placing himself between the men and his students. Unfortunately, unlike Jimmy, who he desperately wished was here right now, Uncle's humour often backfired, making a bad situation worse.

"What?" he said with a toothy grin. "You guys run out of dope? Back for more already?" The five men stared at each other in amazement. Fire and Wood shook their heads, preparing for the worst. Sally and the Chinese students closed ranks.

One of the men spoke up. "What we've come for, old man, is your balls on a plate."

Then another voice made them an offer. "The rest of you can go, and you won't get hurt. All we want is the old man."

"Not a chance," said Fire between clenched teeth. *If these guys are barehanded,* he thought to himself, *they're going to get one hell of a surprise.* Anyway, he wasn't about to let anything happen to Sally, even if he had to use his knowledge of deadly vital striking points which could stop the circulation to a man's heart and which was taught only to senior students for use as a last resort.

Sally for her part was looking around for policemen, but none were in sight. She came to the conclusion that the men had timed this well, and that it was unlikely anyone would be coming to their rescue. Before Kuo could attempt to stall or reason with the men any further, one of them grabbed a switchblade out of his pocket and lunged toward him.

Unlike many martial arts, Taichi, when used competently for self-defence, is relaxed and expends very little energy. If you fight and you're good in Taichi, you are relaxed because "nothing is happening." This implies that the martial aspect of Taichi never resists its opponent. On the contrary, emphasis is placed on following the opponent's movement and matching his or her speed until the center of gravity has been disrupted. At this point, the enemy becomes an unwitting "partner" in a sense, vulnerable to attack and easily manipulated.

The enemy is often subdued by a flick of the wrist, a turning of the head, or a quick shifting of the torso. Sometimes a movement can be so subtle as to be undetected by the naked eye.

Experienced masters of the art seem to merely dissolve upon contact, then reappear with deadly force. To the uninitiated bystander, it might look as if nothing had occurred at all. For the opponent, it's a very different matter. Once he sees how easily he can be manipulated and struck, he realizes that if he continues to attack, he will only get increasingly hurt.

Kuo made a barely perceptible connection between his right hand and his assailant's left wrist, throwing him into an arm lock. He rapidly shook the knife out the man's hand and kicked it into a nearby gutter. He continued pressure on the man's shoulder until he was on his knees howling in pain. The men started to move forward, but Kuo increased the pressure on his kneeling victim and shouted, "Better leave now, or I'll take his arm off right in front of you!"

The men seemed to pause for a minute then scattered, leaving their hapless friend to plead for mercy. Kuo picked him up off the ground. Fire came over and grabbed the man's other arm, pulling him in close. "Next time we see you or any of your buddies down here," he said thinly, "we're going to take care of you personally first." Then he pushed the man down the walkway and yelled, "Get movin'!" after him. The man turned once to look over his shoulder and walked away, clutching his sore arm.

"Well that was a close one," said Uncle cheerily after an audible silence. He put his hand around Fire's neck. "Fire," he continued as if nothing had just happened. "You are...how you say it...you're the man!" Everyone laughed and the group permitted itself a collective sigh of relief.

All the men had fled, including the two Kuo saw at the party. He thought back to the troubling comment Jimmy made earlier about having seen them somewhere before and the incident on the stairs near Jimmy's loft. Did they just happen to be there, or had they come on purpose? He shrugged it off. It was over.

Minutes later, with a squeal of brakes, the subway train came to a halt in front of them. The doors slid open, and they all got on.

Chapter 14

Even with our limited knowledge of behavioural psychology, my brother and I could see Ba Ling showed signs of becoming a troubled young woman.

The signs could have been by-products of an inattentive mother, an alcoholic father, or from having spent part of her life in a foreign country. Or they could have been brought on by other disparities and incongruence in her personality, for instance, the fact that here was a shy, bitterly morbid, yet dangerously attractive young girl who just happened to occupy the body of a martial arts champion.

At any rate, her bubbling personality seemed to be eroding by the moment and getting worse every time we saw her. The last time we did, she was in serious decline, a pitiable creature, lost and obviously in need of some urgent professional care. Once we were convinced that her behaviour was becoming self-destructive, both of us decided to try and do something about it.

My brother and I had gotten wind of something called "interventions" from some pamphlets being handed out at school. In the 1960's, this fairly new concept was just being introduced into the suburbs. Mostly intended for hard core drug users who were slipping through the cracks and no longer willing to communicate with their families, the "intervention method" consisted of friends and family coming to your door, or in some cases let in by another member of the household, and staging a surprise attack scenario that could involve anything from scaring the pants off you to seeing that you got immediate treatment.

Our close knit little Taichi family watched with growing concern as Ba Ling turned first to alcohol then hard-core drugs for comfort and solace.

Metal, though not a serious drug user himself at that point, had been discreetly supplying her with small quantities of marijuana from time to time, bowing, no doubt, to pressure from the many occasions she was to show up banging as his door distraught beyond recognition with a face covered in tears.

A man, whom I instantly disliked, called Norman had been seeing her for a few weeks and then suddenly stopped. The incident resulted in a cataclysmic downward spiral for Ba Ling, whose subsequent binging almost landed her in the hospital.

Fa and I weren't present for the events that followed. Nor were we privy to them. However, since we had had more than a considerable hand in initiating them, we were understandably quite anxious about the results. We finally pieced together a reliable amount of information based on student gossip.

Apparently after one exhaustive afternoon of training, Ba Ling turned the key in her door and entered her living room to discover with immense shock, Mei, my mother, sitting ramrod straight in an armchair looking up at her nervously, followed, as she looked around the room by my uncle, Jimmy, Earth Mother, and my stepfather, Harry Chen, who prompted her to gasp. Then she held her hands up to her mouth and burst into tears. She knew about interventions. She'd learned many things since her first arrival in the United States at barely seventeen. The difference here was that no one present in her apartment that day even approached her peer age group. In traditional Chinese society, this factor alone has the power to completely upend the dynamics of any confrontation. If an elder, or even a friend of the family, tells you do something, you pretty much do it.

Jimmy, after a little persuasion from Uncle Kuo, befriended Ba Ling's landlord. He promised to drum up some rental business for him if he would in turn grant Jimmy access to show some of the apartments. Eventually he obtained a master key which he relayed to my Uncle and who then summoned a hasty meeting with the family. Fa and I passed around the flyers from school with instructions and contact information for various doctors and treatment centers. After that, there was nothing for us to do but wait with heavy clouds of apprehension looming over our heads. Had my brother and I done the right thing by coming to the family and Uncle with all of this? Or would it have been better to have waited, stayed out of it, and let things take their natural course? We decided we had done the right thing, nearly fidgeted ourselves to death in the process, and made everyone swear down to the last man to keep mum about our involvement.

Kuo decided to recruit Earth Mother in the final moments, reasoning that the two women had developed a bond and because he thought the old gal might provide a nurturing influence. His instincts proved correct. It was Earth Mother more than anyone else who seemed able to convince Ba Ling to seek help. She and my mother immediately stood up to comfort the distraught Ba Ling and helped to get her quietly seated. Both women said they would team up to find a good rehabilitation clinic, and my stepfather, Harry Chen, offered to make the arrangements and pay all expenses without Ba Ling having to be concerned with repaying him until some future date. Jimmy offered to furnish transportation whenever she needed it, and Earth Mother offered her services as a counsellor or if she needed a friend to call anytime of day or night. The whole package was tied up in a neat little bow. Everything had turned out well, or so we thought.

Despite our collective efforts, Ba Ling walked out the front door of the clinic with her bags packed on the eve of the day she arrived. She took a taxi to a friend's flat in Soho, where she wound up staying for five days without telling anyone. By the time the clinic had gotten around to notifying us, ten days had already passed. Kuo was furious, both he and the group felt useless and betrayed, but it was during this time that Ba Ling was to receive a letter that would change everything for her and everyone connected to her.

Upon opening the letter, Ba Ling frowned at seeing the masthead of the Beijing Wushu Academy, then followed the page down to find a letter from Coach Xiao Feng hastily scrawled in Chinese characters.

First he enquired of her health, arrogantly stating he felt her sword form was "adequate". He continued on to say that the team would be touring Japan and the U.S. in winter, that they were a girl short, and could she possibly pry herself away from master Kuo's "undecipherable teaching methods" long enough to join them? If so, she would need to contact the school directly, and his secretary, a man simply to be addressed as Po, would make all the necessary arrangements.

There was a vague hint of her receiving some monetary compensation once any profit from the tours had been assessed, but he made a point of assuring her that room and meals would be provided at no extra charge. He harped on for some length about the prestige a top spot on the touring Beijing team could add to her resume at such a young age. In addition, there would be exposure to important contacts and references that would almost guarantee her top billing in future tours if she was to be successful. He said that in the process of obtaining her mailing address from master Kuo's T'ai Chi establishment, he heard disturbing news that she'd been coming to school with alcohol on her breath, in which case it would be best for her not to even think about joining the tour until she had cleaned herself up. He then wished her the best of luck in her future career choices and signed off.

Ba Ling's hands were sweaty and shook as she read the letter. What she didn't know was that Xiao Feng was once again back on the road nurturing his pet project and lifelong ambition which at present only consisted of failed attempts to influence Asian Olympic committees about the desirability of introducing wushu into their Olympic programs. Ever since the Japanese martial art of Judo had found it's way into the Olympics in 1964, Xiao Feng, who's dream would not begin to realize itself until three decades after his death, had been patiently feeding breadcrumbs to potential supporters through his school's wushu demonstrations and by showcasing his most talented protégés. To that end the fattest carrot being dangled in front of Xiao Feng's nose to date were the Japanese. If he was able to impress them with the viability of wushu for the Olympics, it might give him a bargaining chip with which to rally support from the rest of the

Asian Olympic community. Xiao Feng's ambitions would eventually intersect with Ba Ling's in years to come, however, no one was to know that yet. In fact, all of this news unfairly and somewhat unkindly was kept under Kuo and the family's radar for several months while Ba Ling was making up her mind.

By September she had decided to go and dropped the news like a bomb on my uncle and a gape-mouthed Jimmy Chow. Kuo took the news unemotionally, at which Ba Ling was privately flabbergasted, but he confided to us later that he felt as though he'd been hit in the stomach with a rail hammer. The plain fact was that both he and Jimmy were deeply hurt and felt betrayed by the whole affair.

"Silly bitch." Jimmy muttered icily. "This is the thanks we get for all we've done. A slap in the face." Kuo kept it together. He quietly told her not to forget the hours of training they had put in, to make Xiao Feng aware that he bad been grooming her to be a T'ai Chi professional, and that he had every reason to believe that she would turn out to be a great success. He also left a nettle in her stew by telling her that if she chose this path he would be unable to take her back.

Undaunted by this, Ba Ling cleaned herself up as much a possible, packed her bags in November, and headed for the airport with most of my family in tow to say goodbye and wish her good luck. Kuo wouldn't keep his promise never to teach her again, and I, summoning up all my courage, backed her up against a wall near some airport rest rooms and planted a kiss on her. She laughed and pulled away.

"The girls better watch out for you Paulie," she said, gave me a big hug, and ran to the gate to catch her plane. She never did find the culprit who informed on her to coach Xiao Feng, but she had her suspicions. At that moment, I had no way of knowing we would soon see her again, and it was impossible to keep the burning tears from running down my chin.

We weren't the only ones saddened by "Ling Ling's" departure. The students missed her terribly. When questioned about her, Kuo remained mysteriously silent. Then one day, as my brother and I were helping to unpack some office equipment at the T'ai Chi School, the students surrounded my uncle. "Where's Ling Ling? What happened to Ling Ling? Yeah, tell us, Master Kuo!" they chanted.

For the students, especially those who'd been assigned to train with her, Ling Ling's departure was considered a great loss. Her jaw dropping skill with the wushu sword was always a popular topic of conversation. That coupled with a pleasing personality and good looks encouraged an easy bond between her and the students. Over the years she had become a friend and mentor to them in her own right. Her abrupt absence tendered without so much as a goodbye left an aching void in the hearts and minds of everyone at the school.

Kuo put up his hands to silence the din. "All right, all right everyone!" he said, finally giving in. He bit his lip thoughtfully, pausing to contemplate what he was about to say next. "You can be very proud of your colleague and substitute teacher Ba Ling. Although she has experienced many difficulties recently, the Beijing Wushu Team has recognized her talent and made her an offer which she has accepted."

There was a collective gasp, then a tide of questions flooded out. "What kind of an offer master Kuo? Why did she leave without saying goodbye? Where is she now? Is she ever coming back?"

"She left on a plane for Beijing last week, and I'm afraid this is all we know," he said, turning his back impatiently, then added, "School is closed for today," and walked out.

Chapter 15

Meanwhile, as Ba Ling was eyeing her uncomfortable cot at the Beijing Wushu Academy, new events were taking place on the home front. Fire and Sally Waterman gave birth to a seven-pound baby boy and decided to get married.

Some of the students including my brother and I received invitations to the christening, and after giving it some thought, decided to go. After all, it wasn't every day that we would have the privilege of seeing the interior of a Christian Church, and we were ripe for a new adventure, one that we hoped would serve to lift us out of our doldrums.

Most of us arrived late and ushered ourselves in, trying to be quiet. The ceremony had already started, and the priest was attending to the tiny boy, cradling him to one side and dripping water over his forehead with the tips of his fingers.

Fumbling, bony knees made contact with wooden pews, and some heads turned enquiringly at us. The priest raised an eyebrow, temporarily distracted from his Latin mutterings and water drippings by the commotion. When Sally caught sight of us however, she waved and, faking a surprised look, pointed to her tiny new offspring while pinching Fire who waved at us with a sheepish grin on his face.

Towards the end of the ceremony, the priest read loudly in English from the Baptism Ceremony Text with a hollow, nasally sound. "Throughout our lives, we are called upon to make serious decisions...the decision of dedicating you make today is one of the most sacred and significant you may declare...By it you confess your faith and formally dedicate yourself to our creator." In this way, Fire had formally turned his son over to God, although the family had yet to pick the godparents.

When it was over, Fa and I spent approximately the next half hour gazing up at the enormous Church windows and interior of its dome. We felt a hand on each of our shoulders and looked up, startled to see the priest standing quietly over us. After a few moments of frightening silence he asked, "Well, how do you boys like the church?"

He received no answer at first because we were frozen in place, our words choked back in our throats. He decided to try again. "I say, boys, what do you think of our little church here?"

He smiled at his own joke, but all I could think to do was stammer out "w...we think its okay, sir"

"You think it's okay?!" he bellowed. "Those statues were all hand carved from the 16th century and brought over here from Italy, and that large stained glass window over there...." he began but then broke off. "Oh well, just enjoy it, fellas." He turned to walk away then hesitated. "Say, both of you look awfully familiar. You wouldn't happen to be the two nephews of one gentleman who calls himself Kuo Yun San by any chance, would ya?" We felt as though our jaws would drop and smash against the marble floors. He laughed heartily at our reactions.

"His family and mine were old friends way back when I was a kid living around the corner from him in Chinatown. They took him back to China when he was still a small boy, and I never saw him again until I had the pleasure of running into him just recently." He chuckled. "It's funny; we still look the same to each other and just like a couple of foolish old men to everyone else. He's told me a lot about you guys, and when I heard some students from his school were going to be here, I put two and two together. My, but you both look like 'im when he was a very young man. Same level gaze of the eyes, same determination. Makes us all wish for when we were young."

"S...sir," I stumbled, my voice spiking with trepidation. "This is the first time either one of us has been inside a Catholic church."

"Well now..." He smiled, slowly turning away. "Well."

An echo of voices erupted behind us, coupled with some murmurings of ooohs and aaahs among the students as Fire and Sally brought their newly christened son out for a visit. Fa and I ran over to where they were standing. The little boy stretched out his hand as if he were trying to touch all the faces arrayed before him. Then he looked up at his proud Papa as if to ask, "What are they all doing here?"

Beaming irrepressibly, Sally gently lifted the little boy from Fire and held him up in front of all the female students. "We are calling him Sam," she murmured triumphantly, purring over him as if she were a cat that had just been fed some warm milk, beneath that vast ceiling dome and the large white altar candles that seemed to go on forever.

These occasions have always remained as memorable to me and my brother as if we could see them backward in time through a pure liquid drop of mercury. And what of the tall Irish priest we met that day who claimed to know our uncle? The question was how to pry the information we sought from a relative who remained so protective over his past. I decided that the best approach was to be blunt and come right out with it.

"The priest at Sally's church says he knows you, Uncle."

"You mean Bishop Frye?" asked Kuo with a bemused smile on his face. "So he told you....eh? Did you speak to him, Paulie?"

"We know very little, Uncle, except that he said the two of you met when you were kids," I replied.

"Bishop Frye," said Kuo pausing for emphasis, "is considered both a pillar of the community and a treasure to his congregation. You should be honoured to have met such a man; people like him are few and far between in this world, and a better friend you could not ask for in this lifetime." Then he peered down at me through his bifocal reading glasses. "You *were* nice to him, Paulie?"

"Of course, Uncle," I answered quickly. "We were both very polite."

"Good," he shouted, seemingly pleased.

"Yes it's true, my parents brought me to New York City one summer to visit my aunt when I was seven or perhaps eight. Some friends of hers came over with their son one day, and that's how I met young John Frye. We played in the streets almost every day that summer. He was a tough little kid in those days, good with his fists already for such a young boy because his father had taught him how to box, and he looked out for me when we got into trouble with the older kids, which was often. I don't like to talk much about this because it was a bad time for both our families. My father got in a terrible fight with my aunt and her husband, and by the end of the summer, they threw us out into the street. John Frye's parents let us stay with them until we could obtain passage on a cargo ship."

Tears began to well up in my uncle's eyes as he continued. "In those days, travelling overseas was difficult. My father was not rich, and it took us a long time to get home. It was a very uncomfortable trip, and my mother was a frail woman. After many rides in boats, trains, and ox carts, she became very sick and everyone believes this was the reason she died that same winter.

"I never forgot the kindness of John or his family. I wrote him many letters, but because it was hard to get mail out of China successfully at the time, he never received any of them. When Mei got married to your stepfather in the city and moved to Chinatown, she sent me a newspaper clipping that showed a picture of John Frye being ordained as a priest. She asked me if this was the man I had been talking about all those years. I remember when I saw it, I cried my head off.

"Two years ago, I saw him walk into the dry goods store, and it was as if time had stopped. We hugged each other. I told him I was opening up a school, and he told me they made him bishop at his church, and that was it. So now you know, hah?" He slapped his knee shaking me out of my reverie. "Stay friends with this bishop, because he's a good man, and I would like the two of you to get to know each other, okay?"

"Sure, Uncle," I replied. He smiled, eased himself back in his armchair, and lit a cigarette.

Yes, now I knew. Both my uncle's future and his past were indelibly intertwined with the city of lower Manhattan.

Getting to know Bishop Fry would not be the daunting or cumbersome assignment I first envisioned. In fact, it was my mother who ended up initiating our first introduction by inviting him to a small family gathering she arranged at our flat above the store. The bishop had been an irregular customer of hers for several years, and I think Mother considered him something of a flirt.

Refreshments consisted of a deep orange Formosa tea served with homemade almond cookies from a recipe handed down to us by my grandmother. I always tasted various exotic combinations of ingredients as a boy when eating these cookies, but have been unable to identify them to this day. One old uncle on my stepfather's side swore there was gunpowder in them, but I was too smart even as a child to attach any validity to this claim. I was also hesitant when it came to asking my mother about them, who was as vague about my grandmother's recipes as she was about my real father.

Bishop Frye bit into one of the cookies, turning the crumbs thoughtfully over in his mouth with intermittent moans of pleasure as if he were savouring some rare and expensive delicacy. "Mmm!" He exclaimed. "Light...perfectly finished on the outside with just a hint of...er....Indian something or other."

My mother smiled. "Here, Bishop, have some of this tea, made fresh," she continued. "Ever since they got home last weekend, Fa and Paulie have done nothing but talk about the christening of their friend's baby and your beautiful church."

"Mmmmh!" shouted the bishop. "Oh yes, Sally...uh. Davis I believe her name is, and the husband, comrade Kuo keeps referring to as Fire." He chuckled. "I can see where he gets the name, though." He alluded to Fire's immense shock of red hair which, in accordance to style dictates, now reached halfway down his back.

"Yes, well..." went on my mother, "my brother often mentions the kindnesses you have shown to him and members of our family...."

"Nonsense! Not at all, not at all," interrupted the bishop, gesticulating with his hands. "It is your brother's kindness and that of you and *your* family that I'm infinitely grateful for. Did you know that your brother is considered nothing less than a role model to some of our apprentice clergymen?"

Fa began to roll his eyes and look over at me with that familiar look. A few family members in attendance cleared their throats and pretended to look busy conversing or puttering around the kitchen. My mother just smiled her fixated smile.

Uncle Kuo was conspicuously absent from the party, but this minor fact did nothing to prevent the large bishop from extolling his praises, or launching into rambling stories about their mutual childhood experiences at the drop of a hat.

Much like the piece named for him in a game of chess, the bishop was a smooth side-scuttler, who was able to accomplish things with charm and diplomacy where others failed. At that moment, however, I began to see him as more of a pawn, an effort by Kuo to make himself look good in front of the family by using the bishop as a kind of mutual admiration society representative. Though my suspicions of the moment may have been well founded, this turned out to be a shallow view. As I came to know the bishop better, I found his respect and admiration for Kuo to be genuine.

What I didn't know was that Bishop Frye had been looking out for my uncle and the family for some time, ever since he knew of Uncle's return. I wondered how some doors seemed to open mysteriously for my uncle and always ascribed it to his embassy connections. I was wrong.

Further down the road, this somewhat pompous clergyman with tea and crumbs running down his chin would turn out to be a life saver in more ways than one. For now, his disgusting manners and the way in which his eyes roved over my mother's tightly fitted skirt prompted me to temporarily excuse myself. I left Bishop Frye with the other relatives who seemed to find him hugely entertaining and went upstairs to get some air on the outside porch. Looking over the rooftops and the purposeful traffic below, I felt suddenly disillusioned with life.

Several days later, my mother dispatched me to the post office with a key to retrieve some mail that had been languishing in the dry goods store's mailbox for almost a month. I stuck the brass key into the face of a lock that looked as if it had been fashioned before the turn of the century and watched it swing open easily between the greasy hinges.

The box was so crammed full of mail and light packages, they got stuck several times as I attempted to pull them out. At the bottom of the pile was a letter with stained edges and the address hastily scrawled in Ling Ling's unmistakable handwriting. It was addressed to my mother, and one of the edges looked as if it had been pried open. With out realizing it, I had put pressure with my thumb on the very spot where the glue had given way, and the letter seemed to open by itself. Looking over my shoulder to make doubly sure I wasn't being watched, I found that I had already read down half of the first page.

"Dear Mei,

"Sorry it has taken so long for me to write, but I have to be careful because the school reads all of my mail. I hope this letter finds you and Harry both well. Please give him my regards and tell him how grateful I am for his generosity. I do so miss Paulie and Fa, and I hope they are doing well and learning much in school. Does Paulie have a girlfriend yet? Ha ha." I blushed at this sentence. "Anyway, I wrote to tell you that the school here in Beijing is closing down for the rest of the year, but I can't stand it here anymore, and I will be returning to New York in just a month. Is there any possibility I could stay with your family for just a little while, kind Mei?" She promised to be tidy and not make a fuss. "You won't even know I'm there," she insisted. "Anyhow, please think about it. I can't wait to see all your lovely faces again, and soon I shall. Love, Ba Ling."

My heart jumped with excitement. Could it be true? Would she be staying with us for the rest of the summer? Would she be in the spare room next to our room? I decided to keep it a secret from Fa until I knew for sure, but I carried a wonderful feeling inside me that whole day with the promise that, after all these dreary months, things would finally be looking up.

Chapter 16

The glass doors of the airport terminal made a squishing sound when they opened. Out walked a tired and bedraggled Ling Ling. She dropped both her suitcases on the dusty, hot pavement and proceeded to hail a taxi but was brought up short by the sight of Jimmy Chow waiting for her in his car.

Jimmy got out and popped the trunk. "Get in," he commanded. Then once he had pulled away from the curb, he broke the news. "You will not be staying with Mei Chen and her family. I have found an apartment for you and given them two months rent in advance. You can pay me later, when you get a job." Ling Ling was sceptically silent at first, wondering just what type of accommodations the notoriously frugal Jimmy had lined up for her.

After a few minutes she asked, "How did you know I would be here?"

"Your former teacher told me you would be," he replied evenly, meaning of course my Uncle Kuo. They both sat in stony silence for the rest of the ride into the city. Ling Ling decided not to thank him until she had given the place a thorough going over.

The apartment was actually pleasant enough. Someone, possibly the building superintendant, was an obvious fan of potted plants and hanging flower baskets which could be seen in almost every corner and more spectacularly out on the small porch. Jimmy wisely took her over during the day when the light was at its best. I didn't seem the cleanliest of places, but it was a far cry from the Beijing she had just left, and there was a touch of cozyness about it. After examining the rooms and bathroom, she came out with a smile. "Thanks, Jim," she said putting her arms around him. "I owe you for this one."

"You sure do," said Jim, breaking into a grin.

"Rent is due the first of the month in October. Don't forget. I'll go downstairs and have them turn on the water and electric.

"Thanks, Jim," she said again, flopping into a comfortable chair with a dusty old pillow. As the power came on, a dingy, beige air conditioner groaned to life, slowly blowing out warm air.

"Paulie, did you know?" said my mother one day. "Ba Ling has been in town for weeks. She's been staying at the Viking Arms apartments over on West 32nd Street." I thought I would collapse from bitter disappointment. I had been boasting to friends and martial arts students alike for over a month that she would be staying with us. Now I would be made to look like a fool. Possibly, a lovesick fool at that. I was terrified what I'd told them would get back to Ba Ling, or even worse, my mother.

"Is that what she wrote to you about?" I ventured. Mother came out of the kitchen.

"When? What do you mean?" she asked.

"I saw a letter from her in the old store box, addressed to you."

"Oh that," she said, waving a cloth she was using to dry the dishes. "That was nothing; she was just sending us greetings from Beijing."

"Are you sure that's all?" I said between gritted teeth. My face was getting red hot and I had rarely been so angry at Mom for lying to me as I was at that moment. There must have been some reason for her not wanting Ling Ling to stay with us, and I wanted an explanation.

"Why not go over and pay her a visit?" she suggested breezily. "I'm sure she'd love to see you."

"No time," I grumbled, helping myself to one large green apple from a bowl on the dining table and biting down on it hard to keep myself from screaming at her. "Bitch," I muttered ruefully with a mouthful of apple.

"What?" asked my mother.

"I itch," I said. "I'll probably have to take this shirt to the laundromat." We still hadn't purchased a washer/dryer.

"Oh great, will you take some of your father's shirts with you?" she pleaded.

"Sure," I replied, feeling utterly defeated.

The only chance I would have to satisfy my curiosity about the Ling Ling story was to talk with her privately. I plucked up the last of my shaky courage and placed a phone call to her from a neighbouring telephone booth. My right hand shook so badly I could barely hold on to the heavy telephone book, but her name was not to be found in the white pages, and I would have to call information. After having to repeat myself several times, the operator gave me her number, and I jammed some more coins into the slot. Finally, I got a ring. "Yes?" A tired voice sighed into the earpiece.

"Ling...hi...it's me, Paulie." My voice was croaking with fear.

"Paulie is that you?" she asked. "How did you get this number?"

I threw a joke in, hoping it wouldn't sound overconfident. "Oh you know me," I said. "Connections with the F.B.I. and all that." To my surprise, she laughed.

"Where are you calling me from?"

"From my suitcase phone," I said, continuing the farce. "They only let me use it once a day." She laughed a second time.

"When are you and your little brother going to come over and see me?"

"Well Fa's still at school," I lied. He had been home for hours. "But I'm just around the corner, maybe I could come over and see you for a little while, if you'd like."

"Well...." she puffed. "The place is a mess, but sure, come on over. It would be great to see you."

"Great, I'll see you soon then," I said, slamming the phone back on its cradle. I raised the collar of my overcoat around my neck and braced myself to walk against the dusty fall winds that swept through the city until I reached West 32nd Street. I pressed a little white button with no name plate beside it and heard a bell ring somewhere in the building's interior. "Come on up!" a girl's voice barked.

Ba Ling greeted me at the door with a familiar kiss on the cheek, but I was taken aback to see Mrs. Liang, sitting stiff spined as a Japanese school girl on one of the apartment's high backed straw chairs, hands expectantly on her knees. She gave me the usual disapproving look from behind her pinched spectacles.

"Hello Paul," she said. "I just dropped by to give Ling some flowers and a nice box of candied fruit." Her eyes dropped to my mittens, noticing that I had showed up empty handed.

"They look very pretty," I murmured, feeling a pang of shame that I hadn't picked up a gift for Ba Ling myself. What was I thinking? In China it was almost one's duty to bring a gift when visiting a friend. Whether accepted or not, an offer of some sort was looked upon a sign of good breeding and was more or less expected. Ba Ling downplayed the gifts in order to save me some embarrassment.

"I'll put them in the kitchen if no one minds," she said." You can go now if you'd like, Mrs. Liang. Thank you so much for dropping by, but Paulie and I have some catching up to do of a personal nature."

Mrs. Liang stayed rooted to her chair for some time, eyeing me suspiciously. The young girl gently took her by the arm and walked her to the door. "Really," she said. "Everything's fine. I'll call you soon, and I hope we can all see each other again and become the friends we once were."

"That is my fervent hope," said Mrs. Liang.

"It will all work out, you'll see," soothed Ba Ling. "Goodbye now," she said, ushering the elderly woman to the door. I bowed respectfully to Mrs. Liang as the door closed behind her, but she gave me an odd look to the last. "She's from the old school," laughed Ba Ling by way of explanation for the behaviour. "She probably thinks we should have a chaperone. Do we need a chaperone, Paulie?" she teased. I could feel my ears getting hot and asked her if I could have some water.

"I met a French businessman in China, and he gave me some bottles of French water to take home," she said. "It's called Evian.

Would you like to try some?" She had become worldlier since her trip, and I couldn't help wondering what other experiences wealthy businessmen had introduced her to.

"Actually I'll just have a beer." I said, desperate to make a grownup impression.

"A beer, huh?" she asked, eying me with a mixture of amusement and suspicion. "Are you sure your dear mother would approve?"

"Sure I'm sure," I said. "Mom keeps beer around the house all the time for us to drink."

"Well I suppose its okay," she said hesitantly at first, but I was actually surprised when she popped open the can and handed it to me.

"Cool place," I remarked, wandering around and peering over some knick knacks and trinkets she had brought back from her trip. There were some jade beads on a table that looked fake, a collection of tiny ornamental snuff boxes, and a silk scroll with Chinese characters on a wall which I hopelessly tried to decipher then gave up. I took a large sip of beer from the can and let out a gasp of satisfaction as I'd seen my stepfather do.

"Do you really like it?" she gushed excitedly.

"Sure, it's nice," I repeated. "I'm so glad you came by to see me. I don't get too many visitors these days." I didn't answer but moped around the place in silence for a little while longer until she sensed something was up.

She interrupted my train of thought by asking "What's wrong Paulie?"

Caught off guard I found it difficult to hide my disappointment. "Oh...uh...nothing...I just heard that you were going to be staying with us when you got back is all."

"What? Did Mei tell you that?" She was incredulous.

"Just something I heard around...I mean...you know how people talk," I said carefully. "Sometimes they get their facts mixed up."

"Well, you're right. That was the plan, at first. Then your uncle and Mr. Chow insisted I not burden the family and that they would be happy to find me a place."

"You wouldn't have been a burden at all. That's ridiculous," I said.

"Anyway, it worked out well," she said cheerily. "The place is great."

"Yes," I said with my jaw involuntarily tightening. "Uncle can always be counted on to do the right thing."

"Come," she said, taking my hand and pulling me into a spare bedroom. "I have something to show you that will cheer you up." She lifted a long velvet emerald box from a closet shelf and placed it on the bed, undoing the clasps with her beautifully tapered fingers. The box revealed a red piece of satin cloth under which was hid a very intricately carved twin dagger set. The daggers were sheathed in ivory and fitted into one another so that the twin blades were hidden from sight. To the naked eye, it was a mere decorative piece.

The carvings alone were in miniature and astoundingly beautiful. I involuntarily gasped as she pulled them apart, exposing the shiny, small, three and three quarter inch blades. "They're beautiful." I murmured appreciatively, feeling the weight of the two perfectly balanced ivory carved handles in both hands.

I thought back to the moment my uncle dramatically unveiled those cheap toy swords for us when we were kids and suddenly forgave him all his foibles and eccentricities. It was he, after all, who opened the wondrous world of Chinese martial arts to us, a gift for which we would always be grateful and forever unable to repay.

"Wait, you haven't seen the best part yet," Ba Ling carried on gleefully. "Just a minute," she said, disappearing into the bathroom where I heard a rustle of clothing.

Minutes later she reappeared in a tight fitting cheongsam dress decorated with plum flowers and a slit halfway up her thigh. In the bathroom doorway she struck a Jean Harlow pose

90

with one hand on her left hip and the other reaching up the door frame.

"Well?" she asked coyly. "What do you think?" I was speechless. Abruptly there was a knock at the door.

"Expecting anyone?" I asked.

"Nope," she said, looking puzzled. Following her out, I was irritated to see Fa standing in the doorway. His mouth dropped open when he saw how Ba Ling was dressed and peered around her shoulder to see if I was there.

"Hi Fa!" she said, smiling and giving him a gentle pinch on the check.

"What are you doing here?" I asked him sternly. "You're supposed to announce yourself before you come over to someone's house."

"I rode my bike all over looking for you," he said. "Mom sent me to find you; she says she wants you home *now*," he added with a satisfied smirk.

"How did you know where to find me?" I asked, dumbfounded.

"Mom gave me the address. She said you might be paying *her* a visit," he answered, jerking his thumb toward Ba Ling. She laughed, and I turned beet red.

"We have to go, I'm sorry," I said mortified, pushing Fa out of the doorway, "Thanks, I had a great time."

"Sure, Paulie, stop by again," she said. "I'm sorry you guys have to run. Tell Mei I love her, and I miss her, and we should get together for tea one of these days soon."

"I'll tell her," I promised, waving goodbye. I grabbed Fa by the shoulder and hustled him down the stairs.

"Wow!" he gasped when we got down to the street. "Did she get all dressed up like that just for you, Paulie?"

"Shut up," I said angrily. The little cretin had practically ruined a nice afternoon. "I'll deal with you later...and don't go telling any stupid stories to mom about what you think you saw here or else." I warned him. "Get on your bike and be careful getting home...AND TELL MOM I'LL BE RIGHT THERE!" I called after him as he pedaled away.

Chapter 17

A week later I opened the shop door to find my uncle, Mrs. Liang, and Mother chatting. The moment Kuo observed me entering the store, he left the women to carry on their conversation and took me quietly aside. "I understand you paid Ba Ling a visit last week," he began. I nodded. "Did she show you her daggers?"

I nodded again. "Yes, Uncle. They looked small but beautiful and very dangerous."

"You would be right," he huffed. "Jimmy still has scars on both sides of his abdomen from a criminal who pulled the same kind on him in Shanghai. He lowered his voice further until it was almost a whisper. "Did you know that Ba Ling is a silver medalist now, and they are trying to get her to perform in the Tokyo Olympics?"

"No she never mentioned that," I replied, stunned.

"Did you also know that she is still drinking and taking drugs?"

I shook my head. "I think I would have been able to tell..." I began in her defence, but Uncle interrupted.

"Jimmy and I have reason to believe she has gone back to her old habits, and this is why, Paulie, even though I know that you are sixteen and a young man now, I must ask you to stay away from her for a little while," he said, putting his hand on my shoulder. "Will you do as I ask?"

Giving in too quickly as usual, I heard myself saying "Sure, Uncle."

"I've had a conversation recently with Mei and your stepfather," he said. "I may not have many years left, and if you agree, I would like give both you boys some personal instruction in the finer points of T'ai Chi Chuan and its application for fighting." He gripped my shoulders solidly with both hands, looked deep into my eyes, and whispered the remainder of his sentences in Mandarin Chinese, which I was barely able to catch. "I have a few reasons for doing this," he continued. "One, as I have said, I am getting old, and I want to make sure certain things are passed down through the family. There are specific secrets handed down from the oral traditions of our ancestors of which no Westerner may have knowledge, lest they bring harm upon themselves or others."

He explained that the secret formulas and oral traditions were locked in riddles, songs, and poetic verse that could only be brought to life in the hands of a teacher with vast amounts of experience. "I am the last member of a family lineage," he said gravely. "Third in a direct line from the original forbears of the art of T'ai Chi Chuan. It is my fervent hope that you and Fa will eventually become the inheritors of this great tradition, and that you will one day recognize it for the gift it truly is. Secondly, when Ba Ling is able to demonstrate that she is clean and sober for a while and willing act responsibly, I have asked her to help you and your brother polish up your sword routines, and lastly, do you remember the restaurant where I took you and your brother as kids years ago?"

"Sure, Uncle," I said. "The one where you put out the candle at the next table without using your breath; how could we forget?" Secretly the incident had embarrassed me.

"Yes, that's the one," he said. "Do you remember the nice man who came out of the kitchen and offered you boys the chocolate cake?" I nodded. "His name is Arthur Fong. This man is an expert swordsman, an expert with weapons in general. When I met him in China, he was mastering one weapon which you have expressed much interest in, Paulie, the Kwan Dao." I could feel my eyes widening with excitement, now he really had my attention.

The Kwan Dao was a pole to which was attached a wide, heavy blade, much like the halberd the English Beefeaters who guarded the Tower of London carried. It was named for the famous Chinese general Ji Ji Kwan who invented the formidably heavy piece that could penetrate armour and was commonly used to slice off the legs of cavalry horses.

"If you are willing," Uncle continued, "to dedicate yourself and obey all my instructions daily without question, I will see to it that Mr. Fong instructs you in the use of this weapon." He cocked his head back and grinned. "Well? What do say? Do you accept?" My heard leaped at hearing these new developments. Without the full realization of the weight I would be taking on in the coming months, I agreed heartily and in fact probably told him I would be honoured.

There was the added bonus of training with Ba Ling, and I had plenty of time to contemplate in those coming months exactly how her role as my teacher might affect our friendship. For now, I knew Uncle would train me hard. I awoke as if from a dream to the sound of his final words. "By the way," he said. "Ba Ling's daggers, the blades are of Persian origin; they were not made in China, but don't tell her."

"How did you know that, Uncle?" I asked. A smile flitted across his face, and he walked out of the room. Mrs. Liang actually waved to me and smiled for the first time. I waved back.

Getting up early to train before going to school proved both difficult and exhausting. I was beginning to harbour plenty of respect for the martial arts masters I read about who had come by their skill in much the same way; training at daybreak in the senior master's courtyard before shouldering a backpack full of books and trudging to school on foot over steep mountain passes, only to return again to train in the evening after finishing their homework.

Learning T'ai Chi Chuan, however, was unlike learning any other kind of martial art. The pace was slow, yet surprisingly physically demanding. Fa and I already had a bit of a head start, but as we soon discovered, there was much left in store for us. Uncle used to intone that it took two lifetimes to learn Taichi, and I was beginning to catch his drift.

Fa seemed to pick things up at a rapid pace, while I found myself lagging behind. I attributed this to his youthful exuberance, rationalizing it as an excuse, when in reality I found learning the one hundred and eight posture Taichi hand form a deadly, dull grind.

I was, however, privy to the exposure of watching my uncle defend himself against armies of attackers even at his venerable age and knew that it could be used with extreme effectiveness as a method of self defence. Masked somewhere beneath the soft slow movements of old people practicing in the park was a gritty, explosive killing art that included strikes to the eyes, knees to the groin, kicks to the bladder, joint locks, and "death touch" strikes based on acupuncture points that could kill instantly. Paradoxically though, once the opponent realizes that he or she has been robbed of their center of gravity, further escalation of violence becomes futile, and the fight is usually broken off.

"Paulie!" my uncle, the master, yelled. "You're losing your concentration. Go stand in Wuji." Wuji, referred to as "Mabu" at the Shaolin temple, or "Horse Stance," was a double shoulder width stance that the temple monks would stand in for hours at a time to strengthen their legs. After about fifteen minutes, my legs felt as if the skin were being scraped off with a paring knife.

The process of learning the Taichi hand forms is first taught by learning the static postures, which are eventually strung together as if one were to thread a single strand of pearls. Thus, Taichi movement is said to emulate "moving through a string of pearls," or more pragmatically speaking, it makes a graceful ascension from one posture to the next.

My uncle's constant admonitions to "Eat bitter so you will taste the sweet," were beginning to chafe, and I shuddered at the thought of the months that lay ahead. My entire body was beginning to ache. I pondered concepts like "Eat Bitter," which sprang from Uncle's Manchurian warrior side. I thought back to his nomadic ancestors, the feared horsemen of the steppe who lived in such horrifying conditions that a single article of their clothing left in a domicile could visit illness upon an entire family.

These wandering tribesmen, incredibly hardened and impoverished by their way of life, brought one of the largest known countries in the seventeenth century to its knees. They taught the Chinese a lesson they would never forget, penetrating massive walls fortified by huge garrisons and strewing corpses in their wake, visible from the high shimmering dunes of the Gobi desert for distances of several miles. My uncle had inherited a fraction of that legacy through his complicated ancestry. Further digging would uncover a mother and daughter, concubines to the Qing dynasty Imperial Court, with a few Confucian scholars thrown in for good measure.

It always struck me as sort of ironic that I knew more about my uncle's past, for years a subject of banter between our Chinese families, than I did of my own or that of my immediate family. He was something of a legend besides being a drinker, smoker, and a bit of a womanizer. Stories of my Uncle's past always seemed more dramatic and compelling than the few, almost shameful tidbits eked out by my mother about my real father and grandparents.

As usual, he had a way of shaking me out of my dream states with a gentle touch on the shoulder. "All right Paulie, that's enough standing for today. Did you spill rice on the master's floor?"

I shook my head. "Not a grain, sir," I replied. In the interest of helping the student to learn some basic concepts in the study of T'ai Chi Chuan, guided imagery is often used. For instance, in certain positions of standing meditation, students may be asked to close their eyes and envision themselves in the role of a monk holding a bowl of rice before a long dinner table, waiting for the Abbot and other monks to be seated. His instructions are not to spill a single grain of rice on the floor while he waits quietly.

Other visualizations might include pretending to stand with your arms suspended around an invisible tree trunk or peering through both hands as if they were surveying the horizon with a telescope, all this while maintaining the squatting "Mabu," or

"Horse Stance," resembling a horseless rider with his feet planted firmly on the ground.

Further exploration into the mysterious world of standing meditation can lead down a slippery slope into regions some see as mystical or paranormal. It prescribes a method by which Chinese martial artists store "Chi." "Chi," the now fabled Chinese word that seems to adorn everything these days from spa products to health foods, is really a word some Chinese use to describe the vital energy circulating throughout the body and universe, something you are born with that is intrinsically part of you but rarely used. Standing meditation, included in the study of Taichi, is said to give you the ability to harness "Chi" for the use of power behind explosive strike techniques and through diligent practice, make the entire body as impervious as a suit of armour. Some critics and disbelievers tend to dismiss the powers attributable to Chi as folkloric superstition or overactive imagination. But I saw first hand what my uncle was able to do with these practices. He made me a believer within minutes, and I stayed that way.

"All right now, let's see you do the first part of the Yang form," said Kuo, folding his arms and leaning back on the park bench where he had ensconced himself.

After I had barely completed a few moves, he started yelling and chanting at the top of his lungs like a raving lunatic. "No, no...NO, NO, NO! STOP, STOP!!!" I decided to put and end to it before his contorted face turned an even more alarming shade of purple. We were in a public park, and I turned around to see if anyone was staring at us. They were. When I turned back he was pointing frantically down at my shoes. "Look at your feet!" he screamed. I looked down, noting that my feet were not showing the proper degree of separation or alignment and that my rear toe was pointing in the wrong direction, all cardinal sins in the fussy world of Taichi apprenticeship. "First you give me toilet stance," he groaned. "Now this?"

"Toilet Stance," was a term thought up by a humorous master, teacher, and friend of Kuo's, one my uncle had gotten a little too much mileage out of over the years. It referred to people who practiced the Wuji stance incorrectly by splaying their feet outward instead of keeping them parallel to each other, making them look as if they were squatting over a toilet seat. For the moment, I was squirming.

"Sorry, Uncle," I muttered, making the required minute corrections.

Kuo shook his head. "I don't know, Paulie," he said, heaving a sigh. "You're going to have to concentrate much better than this if you expect Arthur Fong to let you touch a weapon like the Kwan Dao." I knew he was right. Every minute I spent training these days made me look like more of a disappointment. It was inevitable. My brain was clouded with thoughts of girls, schoolwork, and occasionally Ling Ling somewhere in between.

Uncle lit a cigarette then sat back down on the bench, waving at me to continue. "Again!" he bellowed.

"Where do you want me to take it from, Uncle?" I asked.

"From the beginning, where do you think?" he replied, his facial expression darkening.

Chapter 18

I awoke to the skittering of young sparrows perched on our roof's drainpipe and hoped I was hearing the first sounds of spring. Starved for a glimpse of sunshine, I bounded out of bed and threw open the double doors leading to our upstairs porch where fog and chilly wind made premature contact with my cotton pyjamas. It was still freezing, and I could barely see my hands in front of my face. I stood there in a light drizzle and fog, clutching the railing with both hands.

About the only thing my senses could discern through the fog were sounds of distant traffic while the birds chirped on. That's how the day started. A somewhat disappointing beginning to be sure, but even as the rain spattered hair stuck to my face, my mood was beginning to lift. I remembered this was the day Uncle had hired Ling Ling to brush up my sword routine and that I still had one more glorious day off from school.

After three months of summer training hell with Uncle and spending the winter boning up for college entrance exams, I had finally earned the right to extract some "sweet" from the "bitter" as Kuo had long ago promised. I had reached certain milestones in my study of T'ai Chi that uncle considered essential. My routines had become so free moving that, as Uncle gloated happily, a fly could not alight on my shoulder without setting me in motion. I experienced a new lightness of being. I could detect thought processes from an opponent in advance. I had learned joint locks where a man could be brought to his knees simply by controlling two fingers and bringing pressure to bear on certain areas of the hand. I had learned to capture or redirect anything that came at me regardless of speed. And I was learning the Dim Mak, the study of bodily pressure points that could stop the circulation, or if necessary, deal someone a killing blow. To put it mildly, I had become unstoppable, or so I thought. The average man on the street wouldn't have a chance.

Of course, I was light years away from the skills of great masters such as my uncle or his teachers. One story my uncle enjoyed retelling from time to time was first told to him by his teacher who spent many summers in the Yang family household, forbears of modern style Yang Taichi. "One day, a servant ran into the garden to wake a Yang family member who'd fallen asleep and to announce that dinner was ready. The Yang brother, still asleep, kicked the poor fellow nearly to the level of the roof!" After the telling of this, uncle would slap his thigh, and between guffaws, mentioned how much he would like to have seen the fellow's face.

Fa, who it seemed was always better able to concentrate than I, and as a consequence always fared better, won my uncle's admiration by successfully passing a series of tests which were more like traps that Uncle set for him. To use an example, on one occasion Fa showed up for his usual training time at the T'ai Chi school and was surprised to find himself one of only three students in attendance. Uncle was just lifting the needle off a gramophone record he had been playing when he suddenly turned and gruffly ordered all three to stand in the corner in Wuji then promptly walked out calling over his shoulder that he would be right back. When he failed to do so, the two other students looked at each other after about twenty minutes, bones aching, and began to wonder aloud what was going on. One by one they left, but Fa remained behind, determinedly holding his position until my uncle returned over an hour later.

Uncle told him he could relax, gave him a fatherly hug, and said, "Fa, I'm proud of you. You have passed a great test today. Always keep faith in your teachers, and always expect the unexpected."

I thought about those words as I glanced down at my watch; it was time to see Ba Ling. Although I knew she probably would show up late, I was resolved to get there on time and be waiting for her. Fa secretly longed to train with her as well and was very disappointed when Uncle assigned him to one of his male senior Chinese students instead. He knew that she was not only beautiful but also a medal winner and contender for the Olympics in Japan. But Fa was still only thirteen, and Kuo was concerned that under Ba Ling's tutelage he might accidentally be exposed to aspects of the adult world which he had no business being exposed to yet. I surmised correctly that uncle trusted my level of maturity more to help me navigate these types of waters. I was only four years older than Fa, barely seventeen, but would have been considered already a man in China; someone who could take on the burden of running and supporting a household with a large family, if necessary.

It was getting late, and I couldn't find one of two swords I needed, my Taiji broadsword. Clothes went airborne out of the closet until I felt a presence behind me. It was Mom, holding the sword. "Forget something? I found it out in the living room. I thought I raised you better than to leave swords lying around all over the house." I blew out a sigh of relief, grabbing it from her, and she put both hands on my shoulders. "Now Paulie...Paulie! Slow down!" But I was already out the door. "Behave yourself, and act like a gentleman with Ba Ling!" she called out. I made as much noise as possible leaving so she wouldn't think I heard.

I burst through the school's double doors surprised to see Ba Ling thoughtfully polishing a sword lying across her angular knees. Her posture was erect, perfect as usual, and her hair looked as if it had just been washed.

She looked up and smiled. "Hi Paulie!" Then she dropped the sword and gave me a hug. It was one of those close hugs women give when they want you to feel the entrance to their vaginas. I had only moments to be taken aback or flustered because after the hour started she was all business.

I began the Chen form first routine awkwardly and somewhat nervously. Her high pitched commands were sharp and crackled as if they were coming from a Communist loudspeaker. "Back straight! Hold the sword higher! No, at chin level! Turn your foot....not that way!"

She leaned into my body as some teachers do when they want you to get the correct feel of a posture by, in essence, letting you mould to them.

She put her arm around my shoulder. "Let's take a minute, Paulie," she said, smiling sweetly. "Your uncle is a great teacher, but he's let you get away with bad habits for too long. Now here's what I'd like to do..."

To my profound shock and disappointment Mrs. Liang showed up at precisely that moment and started banging around one of the outer offices, shuffling papers, and slamming file cabinets in and out to make sure we knew she was there. Ba Ling held her fingers up to her lips and giggled. I just rolled my eyes and decided to keep going till I finished the form, quite proud of myself for a first day, I thought.

"Okay Paulie, listen. I can only be here once a week, so you're really going to have to pay attention to your training in between. Paulie...look at me...promise."

"I promise," I said. Then she made corrections to my postures that at times moved me less than a centimetre. Real masters could do that. I was impressed.

"I have to go," she said, hurriedly picking up her back pack. I nodded and she hugged me again and left.

I sat alone for a while, pondering how to take in the new Ba Ling. The next time around would involve some fencing, and I wasn't quite sure I was up to it. I lit a cigarette, something I would never do in front of my uncle, and placed the gramophone needle on a record someone had left on the turntable. It was Mozart. The sounds of symphony No. 40 in G minor drifted through the training hall. Mrs. Liang was long gone. I finished my cigarette and left.

Chapter 19

So it went with my female teacher and first crush. No slurred speech, no alcohol breath, no withdrawal symptoms, all things I fully expected but hoped I wouldn't be in a position to discover. Only raw nerve discipline stood between her and the habitual cravings.

Ba Ling's first official day back at the T'ai Chi School several weeks earlier turned into an event. The students fussed and cooed over her. "Oh Ling Ling...Ling Ling!" they chorused. "So great to see you. How was China?" She put on a brave smile, but looked gaunt and tired as if she'd been through the mill. The gin mixed with heroin mill to be precise.

She and Earth Mother hugged each other for a long time. They had been corresponding while she was away, and something else I didn't know was that members of the student body had been pitching in on her behalf. Metal drove her to rehab and A.A., doing an about face in his role as supplier. Sally and Fire tried to fix her up with a friend of theirs and were paying her regular visits. Earth Mother sprang for the odd dinner or two, and Uncle secretly advanced her money through Jimmy, but she was just getting by. My stepfather gave up on her, having not seen a cent since he financed her stay in rehab over a year ago.

One night, at about two o'clock in the morning, Jimmy Chow received a desperate phone call. It was Ba Ling, asking if he could come over right away and whether or not he had a spare key to her apartment because she was too weak to come to the door. After rousing the landlord from a drunken slumber, Jimmy obtained a key and burst into the room, closely followed by the landlord who frantically waved his hands about and began jabbering in Hunanese. "The girl is trouble, always trouble," the landlord kept repeating. Jimmy handed him a fifty dollar bill and pushed him out the door.

He found Ba Ling sprawled on her couch, throwing up in an ice bucket. He immediately got to work, rounding up anything that smacked of alcohol and pouring out the contents. Perfume bottles, nail polish remover, and turpentine were some of the items he emptied into the sink along with a bottle of vodka he found behind her refrigerator and a pint of gin half finished that he pulled out from beneath one of the sofa cushions. Then he went through her medicine cabinet, confiscating all her prescriptions, transferring them to a paper bag, and locking them in the trunk of his car. Donning a pair of gloves he fished around some more, muttering as he came across two cellophane bags of brown junk taped to the underside of a drawer and a pair of used syringes still stinking of residue which he also confiscated. Even in her half drunken stupor, Ba Ling knew that Jimmy was just following instructions given to him by one of the clinic's attendants. He would take care of her.

After about half an hour, Jimmy determined that he had better take a weak and bloodless Ba Ling to the hospital. In addition to the fallout from the booze and pills, it seemed as though she may have contracted a case of food poisoning. She would make a complete and speedy recovery, but word leaked out, and other similar events branded her as a bit of a problem.

So it went that in light of these and other troubling incidents, everyone was pleased beyond belief when she sauntered back into the school on her first day since returning to New York, replete with backpack and sword strapped neatly to her shoulders. Although pale and several pounds lighter than I remembered, she looked ready for business.

Actually, I'm not certain how it happened, but my infatuation with Ba Ling slowly waned as a carousel of young women slowly began their parade through my life, though my admiration for her never would. Deep at her core was a molten steel resolve, responsible for making her a champion, and I envied her that. I still hadn't found my calling and was older than she was when she'd found hers. It was perhaps the hours spent as her pupil that had turned lust into admiration, or perhaps simply that my lust had run its course and was beginning to fade before other youthful distractions.

At any rate, as uncle promised, the time had now come to focus my attentions on learning the Chinese halberd with Arthur Fong, the prodigious weapon I had dreamed of mastering. I had been invited over to his house, and when I got there, Jocelyn, his wife, answered the door. She wore no makeup but was still unbelievably striking and young looking. My uncle had been carrying a torch for her over many years, but as far as I knew, they never had any intimate relations.

She was smiling. "Hello! You must be Paul, or is it Paulie?" she asked. Her voice sounded almost musical. "Are you thirsty? Can I offer you something to drink?" she continued, quizzing me earnestly as I came inside and stared up at the thirty foot high ceilings supported by massive oak beams.

"No thanks," I answered in a flat monotone, consciously intimidated by my foreign surroundings. "I'm here for a lesson with your husband. I can get something later at school."

"Sure, okay," she said, still smiling. "But if you need anything, just ask. I'll go get him for you." I nodded a silent reply, taking in the rest of the room with its huge couches, overstuffed chairs with ottomans, a lengthy rug made out of zebra hide, and a giant size television set. A number of trophy animal heads lined the walls, among them a water buffalo and an African gazelle with horns reaching up to the ceiling stared down at me imposingly.

She ushered me toward the rear of the house, into a mossy courtyard. A stone fountain tinkled in its center surrounded by potted trees and tall exotic plants, offering a shady reprieve from the sunlight poking through. I was left alone for a rather long and anxious wait. It had rained the night before, and the ground felt slippery beneath my feet. *Is this where we are supposed to train?* I thought almost out loud to myself.

My thoughts wandered to the unrequited relationship between my uncle and Jocelyn Fong, and I wondered if any parallels could be drawn between it and my almost completely one sided affair with Ba Ling. Had Uncle felt any of the same strangeness I wrestled with? The unknowing of it all? Whether one of the women he truly cared for in his life ever had any real feelings for him, but he could never bring himself to find out? For my part, as I began to mature, I realized that Ba Ling was probably gaming me for her own amusement or out of sheer boredom. But perhaps there had been some genuine give and take between Jocelyn and my uncle. At any rate, it was some kind of secret between them he would take to his grave.

As I pondered these things, Arthur Fong sprang from the surrounding foliage like a lion out of the Serengeti brush. "Catch!" he yelled, hurling a large pole with a sharp object attached to the end of it at face level. As I caught the huge Chinese halberd, or Kwan Dao, with both hands, I was stunned by how heavy it actually was. Was I really going to be able to master a weapon this demanding? My old insecurities returned in force. Sensing my thoughts of unease, Arthur beamed a huge grin. "Perhaps this is too much weapon for you," he said, snatching it deftly out of my hands before I could blink. "Come on over here and show me what your Uncle and his charming young assistant have been teaching you about the art of Chinese swordsmanship."

Oh great I thought, here's a master Katana swordsman who spent years under both Chinese and Japanese masters about to shoot holes through my pitiable little sword routine. I felt like a calf recoiling before a branding iron. Arthur sat on a stone bench, unwrapping two swords that he had brought down with him, a jian, the Chinese straight sword, and the fatter broadsword. They were both exquisite examples of early craftsmanship. Knowing it would be a bit easier and hoping it would loosen me up and give me a chance to relax a bit, I asked if I might start with the slower broadsword routine. "Let's see what you can do with the jian first," he countered. "Try the Chen...uh...first routine."

He placed the Kwan Dao carefully on one of the stone benches within the limits of my vision. The curved edge of the enormous blade winked at me in the sunlight. The blunt edge was ornately engraved, as was part of the pole on which it rested. Nine rings were often attached to the blunt edge, which made a rattling sound designed to intimidate the enemy. But these were usually found on the ordinary, cheaper Kwan Daos the monks used to practice with. The striking weapon I was looking at was probably worth thousands of dollars or may have been priceless. Even the two gorgeous swords Arthur brought down with him had been signed by their makers in Chinese characters. I couldn't help but marvel at the sheer quality of these instruments of death, but they were not of Arthur's prime stock, and he seemed to take them for granted.

I couldn't help wondering how he had come into the possession of so many fine pieces of exotic craftsmanship. When I thought about the battered cheap swords and poor equipment passed around at uncle's T'ai Chi School, I felt a bit sad for the students. Most would have given up long before this point anyway. *What a shame*, I thought, *never to have held a truly good quality weapon in your hands after putting months or in some cases years of effort into studying it.* I put these thoughts aside and began the Chen sword routine.

Arthur wisely picked a sword for me of correct weight only after consulting with uncle Kuo about my approximate physical statistics. The jian was light, perfectly balanced, and swooshed quietly through the air when it was time for it to perform. I felt as if I was being led by it through the entire routine. When I was finished Arthur smiled. "Not too bad," he offered.

At the time, I lacked one vital piece of information about Arthur Fong which I later exploited to its fullest extent. It had to do with the fact that, although Arthur was a master Japanese swordsman, he really knew very little about the use of Chinese weapons, having only been taught the hand form by his Chinese master. His instruction in the Kwan Dao had been sort of a fluke, and I ultimately learned that he only taught me half of one of the forms.

Still, at the moment, I was sweating, which was something that went against the grain in my uncle's camp.

"Never let them see you sweat during a T'ai Chi sword form," was not only Kuo's motto, but he felt sweating could only be the result of improper practice since one was meant to stay relaxed at all times. Whenever he saw a student sweating, he would politely take them aside and tell them to take a break until they cooled off.

Chapter 20

Arthur was taught the Kwan Dao by a one-eyed lunatic who once claimed to have been a priest kicked out of the Shaolin temple under false pretences. The man was eventually found beaten half to death by a group of Chinese warlords. When Arthur later attempted to check his background, he ran into nothing but dead ends. Most unsettling of all was that the man's credentials appeared to have been deliberately falsified. Yet Arthur was somehow convinced or duped into believing that this one eyed tyrant, who forced him out of bed at three in the morning and lived on a diet of rice gruel scraped from a filthy pot in which it was usually frozen, was one of the most remarkable masters he had ever come across. "Oh what a maniac he was!" Arthur would groan after finishing stories of one hair brained encounter after another with this individual. He placed his hands on the sides of his temples. "It makes my head hurt just thinking about him." Then he would exhale loudly, sighing, "But man was he good."

"So come, Paulie," he said, motioning me to sit. "Tell me, how goes it with your uncle and the rest of your family. I think Mei has been to my restaurant once. Please tell your entire family we hope to have the pleasure of another visit again soon."

"Uncle is fine," I said measuredly. "And my parents both work, so of course they are very busy."

"Of course they are," said Fong, clearing his throat. "But everyone needs a bit of recreation now and again. I'm sure your mom could use a break from the kitchen for one night, eh?" he said, giving a sly look and elbowing me in the ribs.

"I'll pass on your invitation," I said stoically, recognizing one of the routines Arthur used to drum up a little business for himself. He rarely missed an opportunity, a fact that stretched to include all areas of his life. I felt I could learn a lot from him in that regard. I had already missed so many in mine.

"Now," he went on, picking up the Kwan Dao. "I'm sure you have heard all the usual stories about this weapon being used by foot soldiers against cavalry to slice off the legs of the horses and so forth...blah, blah, blah. The fact is that in the proper hands, it was more like a killing machine on the battlefield. The first Gatling gun, so to speak." I knew he was referring to the first "machine gun" invented during the American Civil War, one of the first weapons of "Mass Destruction."

"Equipped with one of these weapons and properly trained, a soldier could inflict many casualties at once," Arthur remarked gravely. As it turns out, the Chinese were far ahead of their time even during the period of this weapon's development. They had already begun experimenting with gunpowder and explosive devices set to detonate on the battlefield, taking out scores of their counterparts.

"In the beginning move of the Kwan Dao routine, you must hold it first like so and then help it along by giving it a slight kick upward with the foot so that it comes to rest in both hands pointing straight ahead. Like this." Arthur gave an impossibly graceful demonstration. I mimicked him through the first move, slowly at first, then gradually picking up speed. I actually did pretty well. "Bravo!" he exclaimed. "You're a natural."

This is going to be easy, I thought, failing to anticipate the hard work that lay ahead. The remainder of the routine he taught me turned out to be as frustrating as it was intricate, and it would be seven long months before I had even begun to feel anything approaching mastery. Arthur was patient but often took to practicing Aiado while I was going through the Kwan Dao routine which threw me off unmercifully. Aiado, a Japanese sword practice, featured a Samurai move that required one to draw and cut through the air from a kneeling position in one single motion. The lightening transitions from kneeling to standing were accompanied by sudden bloodcurdling yells and theatrical facial expressions, which coming from the likes of Arthur Fong, could be very unsettling.

On mornings that didn't mandate my attendance in class, we took breaks while Jocelyn served us tea. Arthur usually had a small silver flask whose contents he poured into the tea whenever Jocelyn wasn't looking, and like uncle, he also smoked cigarettes.

After a few sips of piping hot emerald brew which contrasted sharply against the sparkling white china, conversation usually turned to my uncle, about the only subject we had in common.

"Did your uncle ever tell you of our first meeting?" Arthur asked one day. I shook my head, unable to speak over a mouthful of hot tea and an almost entire slice of spiced apple cake Jocelyn portioned out for us.

The wind picked up slightly and the leaves rustled in their coolness.

"I had just rented a place in Hong Kong, and I was starting up a school for Japanese sword," he began. "Of course, this was a century ago when I was in my late twenties," he added, chortling. As I look back, I remember thinking that being in one's late twenties was already pretty old. By that time I hoped to have accomplished the major portion of my life's work, whatever that might have been. How naive I was.

"Anyway," Fong continued. "One day, in walks your uncle with a short tough kind of guy named Jimmy." *A sidekick even then*, I thought to myself. "We had a silly student there at the time named John Wang who used to practice throwing kicks at almost everyone who came through the door though I had many times tried to get him to stop." He paused for a sip of tea then resumed. "The nature of your uncle's visit was supposed to be one of simple courtesy. He had heard about my school, and both men came over to introduce themselves and wish me well. Also, I thought, to check up on me to see how well I was doing with enrolment and so forth."

That would be typical, I thought. I agreed with him but said nothing.

"Your uncle would have been about in his mid-thirties by then, and seemed frail. I never saw the man eat anything substantial. My God, his wrists looked about the size of napkin rings! Anyhow, back to this guy, Wang. Wang for some reason, and please don't ask me to analyze the reasons for his behaviour, because I couldn't do it in a million years, looked, as I said, at everyone that came through that door as a challenge. No sooner had we all shaken hands, then this fellow comes over and says something or other to your Uncle, trying to get him into a fight. I immediately walked over to him to tell him to cease and desist, and right then, he backed up and threw this roundhouse heel kick at your Uncle's face."

I smiled. I had seen this type of attack levelled at Kuo before; the guy was definitely toast. "And your Uncle" he went on, stifling a laugh which caused him to sputter through a mouthful of tea, "Traps this guy's leg in a sort of Chinese kickboxing move and sends him flying through the air, all the way to the other side of the room, smashing one of my mirrors to bits. Now, the mirrors I had in that studio weren't easy to come by in China, and I had paid dearly for them out of my own pocket." He laughed. "Well, the expression on Wang's and the other students' faces was priceless, but I was pretty angry at the time, and I remember shouting at your Uncle something like, 'Who in the hell is going to pay for all this!?'

"I remember him calmly telling me that it would be replaced the next day, but I didn't believe him and told him to get out. I was furious mind you. So the next day, I'm unlocking the door to the school, and out of the corner of my eye I see something laying flat on the floor wrapped in brown paper. Somehow your uncle had arranged for a deliveryman to meet my landlord in the middle of the night, and right there was a brand spanking new mirror sitting on the floor. You could have bowled me over with a ping-pong ball. From then on, we became immediate friends, even dated a few of the same girls," he said, following the curves under Jocelyn's apron out of the corner of his eye as she picked up the tray and walked back into the house.

Then he cupped a hand over his mouth and drew closer, whispering, "But I got the pick of the litter." He laughed mirthfully between crumbs of yellow cake. I joined in the laughter, but felt a pang of sadness and empathy for my uncle. Jocelyn rarely even looked at him. Whenever I saw her and my uncle together, they were at best civil to each other. Now with the addition of my uncle's new wife, Mrs. Liang, the weather grew even colder between them.

Chapter 21

When you threw in Ba Ling's tutelage and Arthur Fong's courtyard of higher learning with schoolwork, there was precious little time for extracurricular activity, let alone the basics of eating and sleeping, but somehow I managed to find a way.

During that summer, the T'ai Chi School suddenly became infiltrated with people in tights and leg warmers. Sensing the perilous nature of the school's accounts, Uncle had decided to rent studio space periodically to a group of students from the New York City Ballet. The students turned out to be from an elite corps that was renowned for training together and learning from each other.

Young women in leggings and pantyhose were running down the hallways. Fa and I watched in awe as they shouldered their knapsacks to catch a bus or skimmed between us and the walls on the way to a late rehearsal. Sometimes in the evening hours, a tall muscular black man could be seen performing a solo routine. He did pirouettes and plies with equal ease and twisted himself into poses that looked as if they could do bodily harm. His posture was erect and his muscles glistened with sweat. Fa and I welcomed the school's transformation, even though it was only a temporary one, and of course, there was this one girl. Her name was Blythe, and her parents lived in the Hamptons. She took dance as an elective and stuck it out mainly because she enjoyed being around the group.

I found the dance group fascinating myself and discovered that T'ai Chi students and dancers often enjoyed practicing together. It was at one of these informal get-togethers between dancers and students where everyone felt relaxed and able to express themselves, that I met Blythe. When I first saw her I walked in and immediately became one with a group of students going through a familiar martial arts routine, but it was hard to take your eyes off of her. She stood in a corner of the room by herself, doing slow pirouettes, tying and retying her ballet slippers, and stretching her legs. We made brief eye contact during a break, after which I decided to brew a pot of coffee out of my uncle's electric coffeemaker. I walked over and introduced myself with a simple "How are you? My name is Paul," and handed her a cup of coffee. She seemed grateful, cupping it with both hands and taking a sip. I offered her milk and two sugars, but she politely waved it away. I was starting to like her already.

I asked her how long she'd been with the ballet. She said she wasn't officially a member, and launched into a story about how, after giving an audition for the New York City Ballet, she was briskly informed that there were no more spots left but caught the eye of a principle dancer named Jarrod who was forming his own dance company and asked her if she wanted to try out. She said the idea intrigued her so much that she dropped some of her college courses in order to pursue more time with the group. She added that they had been having difficulty finding rehearsal space until my uncle came up with his offer. When Jarrod learned the T'ai Chi school had been a dance studio, he immediately forked over a cash advance into my uncle's eagerly awaiting hands. That's how she came to be here, she said.

"And how about you? How long have you been studying the martial arts? You seem very accomplished," she flattered, continuing to sip her black coffee. Blythe was the sort of girl that had classic dancer's features, the long graceful neck, tapered but firm leg muscles, and wavy blond hair pinned up in the back. I replied that my uncle was actually a famous master from China and that I had been studying with him since I was little. That wasn't quite true, but at least it gave the impression that I was devoted to my craft.

"Wow! A master. Does that mean he's a really good teacher?"

"Well basically, yes," I started to explain, but Jerrod interrupted us.

"Blythe, everyone's left. If you don't want to miss the Nureyev rehearsal, you better get going," he added authoritatively. Then he turned to me. "Hey!" he said, extending his hand to introduce himself. "I'm Jerrod. You don't mind if we borrow your friend here for a little while do you? I promise we'll bring her right back." He finished the sentence with a wry smile, putting a sweater around Blyth's shoulders and escorting her out of the room.

"See you later, Paul. Nice meeting you," she said with a flirtatious look back. I could only put up a shaky hand to say goodbye. Our first date, oddly enough, would take place at Arthur Fong's house.

In those days, working after hours at the store barely yielded enough to do much with except buy a new pair of jeans. Fa and I were not permitted to have allowances, so I wasn't carrying around a lot of cash, and I badly wanted a date with Blythe. I thought about Jocelyn's offer to have dinner with her and Arthur sometime and "Bring a friend if you like." I dismissed it, then thought about it again as I ran into the girl one week later.

We almost rammed into each other coming around a street corner in Greenwich Village. For her it was a battle between groceries and a pile of books she was hugging to her chest. The groceries won and her books spilled out into the street. As I scrambled to pick them up, I still hadn't realized it was her.

"I'm so sorry," I blurted out, angry at my own clumsiness and inattention. I caught myself staring up into a very intent looking pair of green eyes. They seemed to be battling rage with amusement.

"Oh, hi!" we both said at the same time. Blythe was breathless and on the go as usual, looking fantastic.

I started to apologize again, but she cut me off. "I thought only clumsy morons hung out around T'ai Chi studios," she said. We laughed, and I decided right then and there to ask her out on a date. I said something to the effect that I thought she had suffered enough with my uncle's morning coffee and I wanted to make it up to her. "Yeah, stuff's pretty bad," she agreed. We both laughed again, and I asked her what she was doing Saturday night, and if she'd like to meet at a local coffee shop. "Sure, okay," she said, running away.

"I'll see you at Al's about seven!" I called out sharply, but she was gone. I was left with only the hope that she wouldn't stand me up. I pictured myself alone in a dark coffee shop, waiting helplessly for her, and tried to drive it from my mind.

When I arrived at Al's Coffee Emporium precisely at seven, Blyth was already sitting at the counter chatting up a couple of girlfriends. She smiled as soon as I came in the door and waved me over. "Hey girls, this is Paul," she said, putting a hand on my sleeve and tugging me closer to her.

"Hi," I said. The two girls gave me a quick appraisal, and finding nothing of interest, turned back around to continue their conversation.

"Hey Blythe, why don't we get a table?" I said, lowering my voice. "Would your friends like to join us?"

"I don't think so," she said. "They're waiting for someone." Then she put her hand on the shoulder of one of the girls, a luscious brunette, probably also a dancer. "Hey Pam, I'm gonna sit with Paul for a minute, okay? You're welcome to join us later if you'd like."

"Okay, great," the girl said quickly, continuing her conversation almost as though she hadn't heard us. We took a seat by the corner window. Blythe made a show of unwrapping a long scarf that wound about her neck, allowing her hair to fall softly just below the shoulders of a chocolate turtleneck sweater. The waitress arrived on cue and asked us if we wanted anything.

"Two regular coffees, black," Blythe said, looking over at me with a smile.

"I'll have a Danish too," I said, suddenly feeling the need to fortify myself before I got around to asking her the big dinner date question.

"And I'll have a whole grain muffin," she added, fishing around in her pockets. "I've got this," I said, handing the waitress three dollars and fifty cents and telling her to keep the change.

The waitress was unimpressed, but Blythe murmured appreciatively with an amused smile on her face, "Hmmm. Big spender, eh?"

"When I'm trying to look good in front of someone from the Hamptons, you bet," I answered a bit drily. She laughed. A good sign. "Did you grow up there?" I asked.

"My parents divorced when I was little," she said. "My baby sister and I live in the house they left us with my aunt." We made small talk as I watched Blythe eat her whole grain muffin in small bites

After some more talk about our families, I decided to take off my boots and wade into the deep end. "My uncle has this friend from Japan who owns a restaurant in town," I began uneasily. "They have this huge house with stuffed animal heads all over the walls and a dining room table as big as my family's living room. His wife invited me and a guest over for dinner, and I was wondering if you'd like to come."

"What does this guy do?" she asked.

"He's a Japanese swordsman," I answered.

"Great," she said. "I'd love to come."

Chapter 22

Her reply stunned me into silence, but a week later, there we were, standing in the middle of Jocelyn's beautifully decorated foyer surrounded by Japanese porcelain urns. I already informed my mother that I had a date and that we would be having dinner at the Fongs'. When she pressed me about it, I said as little as possible and quietly walked out. Jimmy agreed to drop us off in his old Volkswagen, by now a puttering smoky heap which he refused to give up on. After a white knuckled ride, he offered to pick us up as well, but to my profound relief, Arthur told him he would drive us both back in his Cadillac

Jocelyn greeted us at the door as usual with a big fanfare, giving us a hug and ushering us into the living room. I caught Blythe doing exactly what I did when I first came there, staring up at the wide black face of an African water buffalo and appraising the tusk of a menacing looking rhino jutting out from above the mantel piece. The wildebeest and the African gazelle were still there, looking down as disapprovingly as ever. When I caught Blythe staring at them, we both glanced at each other and smiled. I gave her a look that said "Told ya."

"Would you kids like anything to drink?" Jocelyn asked. "You have two choices, iced tea or Coca Cola." We both opted for cokes as Blythe started off the conversation, asking Jocelyn how long she and her husband had lived there. A maid brought two cokes in on a sterling silver tray. I started to rise, as was my habit around grownups, when the maid came into the room, but Jocelyn waved me back down. Taking the Cokes off the tray and setting them down in front of us, she smiled sweetly at the maid. "You can go home now, Joyce," she said. The maid looked visibly relieved. I watched her don her coat and disappear quietly out of a rear kitchen doorway.

"Arthur and I have lived here nearly nine years...." Jocelyn began in reply to Blythe's question, but the rest of her answer was drowned out by the tidal wave of Arthur's booming voice and grand entrance in an oversize brown dashiki and sandals. The appearance was that of some exotic tribal leader, reaching out for a fresh martini being served to him by his lady in waiting, Jocelyn.

"Well, well, well, well," he carried on loudly. We both stood up and he gave us a warm handshake. "Always great to see you, Paul, and this must be Blythe." I looked over at Blythe. Whatever charm Arthur possessed manifested itself in full force at that moment, and she was hooked. "Please, everyone sit," he commanded. "Welcome to our humble home."

He took a serviceable quaff from his martini glass and continued. "Blythe, Paulie tells me you're a college girl. How on earth is a young woman like yourself able to manage a full time dancing career with the workload they're giving college students these days?" Blythe was being put on the spot by the question, and she knew it. Arthur was trying to determine her level of commitment to education which he always deemed more important for young people than artistic pursuits. No shrinking violet, Blythe confidently returned the serve, telling Arthur that she was taking only the courses required for a bachelor's degree and that she had eliminated almost all extracurricular activities. She also said dance was her real lifelong passion, something with which she could make her parents and friends proud.

Jocelyn excused herself and then came back and stood in the hallway to announce dinner was ready. "Hope you like Chinese food," Arthur joked, giving me a wink. "It seems my wife and the maid have prepared something interesting for us. Please come into the dining room."

"Wow!" Blythe gushed as if the wind had been knocked out of her. "You weren't lying, Paul!" She traced her slender fingertips along one corner of the immense dining room table.

"Fashioned from one single piece of Burmese teakwood. The tree gave its life for the legs too, nothing was wasted," Arthur chimed proudly. Jocelyn wisely decided not to throw a tablecloth over it, but she could still do a table setting right out of Better

Homes and Gardens. The look was splendid on a scale tipping towards ostentatious. On top of that, a wild looking feast lay before us, of which I could identify nothing.

"Is this Chinese food?" I asked as politely as possible once we were seated.

"Well some of it is...." Arthur replied slowly, easing back into his chair with a satisfied smile. He had us where he wanted us. "It's actually a mixture of some different things from different places..." he began then changed the subject. "Paulie, have you or your delightful companion ever savoured the exotic taste of lion's meat? In particular, the head?" He almost looked disappointed as we shook *our* heads in fear. "How about frog legs? Snakes? Small birds or insects of any kind?" Blythe stuck out her tongue and shuddered.

"Arthur," Jocelyn said in a warning tone.

"Just kidding, kids," Arthur carried on gaily. "Actually, it's all Chinese, but some of the dishes come from rural China, and some recipes were handed down to us through families that are centuries old, so you may be unfamiliar with some of them, Paulie. Makes life interesting, eh?" he said, rubbing his hands together gleefully.

Interesting perhaps, but this was my first date with Blythe, and on first dates you don't want anything to go wrong. Gazing apprehensively at the various completely inedible looking dishes and small pots spread out before us, I prayed that there was something we would be able to get down. Upon closer examination, I found the dishes to contain a few ingredients with which I was familiar with, but paired off with rather unusual counterparts.

Stir fried squid were soaking quietly in a suspicious looking dark bath with pieces of black eel. Then there was fish stomach, fried lotus root, the face of some animal I'd rather not describe dismembered from the neck down, and a disgusting looking tofu salad. I was beginning to wish we'd gone to a burger joint. Blythe seemed almost to be jumping out of her skin with enthusiasm, completely enthralled by Arthur Fong and anything he might be ready to dish up. I needn't have worried. Some of the food tasted better than it looked. What was more, Blythe seemed to thoroughly enjoy her role, bravely sampling everything and questioning its origin. I was actually proud of her. She behaved herself beautifully, and her table manners were impeccable. After a few lessons guided by our irrepressible host, she had even managed the art of chopsticks. Fong looked over and winked at me occasionally as if to say, "You picked a winner, boy."

The evening was beginning to turn into a success, and once some of the unfamiliarity had worn off, I settled back and began to enjoy myself. Arthur was just getting warmed up. "Blythe," he began. "Did you know that Paul's uncle is a legend? A kind of very famous martial artist?" I wanted to put up a hand and beg to him not to go down that road, but he was unstoppable.

"Well," Blyth replied, her brow furrowing as she tried vainly to steady a piece of eel between her chopsticks. "He did say something about it." She looked over at me and smiled, "About his uncle being a master or something. Paulie is so mysterious, he never tells me anything."

"Not just any master," Arthur carried on gravely, his bonds loosening from a third martini. "Some say he uses magic, but it's just that the man is so skilled, it surpasses a person's ability to reason properly, and that's why they come up with this bizarre explanation. But it's all quite real, I can tell you. He was a grand champion. When I visited him in Beijing, his medals and trophies were all over the walls, you couldn't move without knocking something over." I reasoned these were items he must have carefully hidden, for I never saw them.

"They called him Style Bearer, or Gatekeeper, or something like that," Jocelyn, who had been sitting quietly observing up till to now, interjected in a faraway voice. She got up to pour her husband a glass of wine. I was a little stunned that she would reveal a family secret of ours like that in front of a total stranger about a relative of mine she evidently still cared for. It almost felt like an imposition. Even Blythe whom I had trusted implicitly up to that point would be owed an explanation later.

"What dear? Ah yes," said Arthur, clearing his throat and giving me a slightly worried look. He appeared stunned as well.

"Wow," said Blythe. "That sounds pretty far out; I'm impressed."

"Oh yes, it's all in the family blood," Arthur continued undaunted. "Paul's uncle sent him to me to learn the Kwan Dao."

"The what?" asked Blythe. "That," he said, pointing to a far corner of the wall where two ornate ones hung, crisscrossing each other. She looked over at me incredulously.

"That's what you're studying?!" Her mouth was agape. "The thing's huge. It looks bigger than you are," she commented. Feeling self-conscious and a little slighted, I straightened myself up in the chair in an attempt to look taller. Fortunately, she didn't ask for any further explanation, and I was much relieved when Arthur changed the subject. I never got around to telling her I had been Arthur's student prior to our date.

"You know, as a very young man, I found work on board Japanese fishing trawlers, and that was long before my involvement with the martial arts or the restaurant business," Arthur waxed on. *That's why his hands felt so calloused,* I thought. Arthur had experienced a hard life from an early age. "We would board the vessels at four in the morning and sometimes not return until nightfall. It was the most punishing work I've ever done."

"What did you catch?" asked Blythe, politely curious.

"Tuna!" boomed Arthur. "Giant blue fin tuna whenever we could. As big as your boyfriend there or bigger!" he said, nodding over at me and winking again. "The biggest ones could be measured from the ceiling to the floor of this house, and sometimes they weighed up to a thousand pounds or more. It took at least six of the burliest men you've ever seen to cut and prepare those monsters and throw them down into the hull where they were frozen solid for the rest of the trip. I was just a scrawny little kid then, but I learned fast, and you had to with that crew. Fish that size always paid good money when they were brought in." Anyone would think he was exaggerating, but I knew better. I had often heard tales from my stepfather, Harry Chen, a former dockworker, about the catches brought in on commercial fishing boats from that part of the country. Even back then, Harry knew it wouldn't be long before commercial fishing would make the giant blue fins and many of the other undersea creatures scarce. While still only a child, I often heard him complaining about it. I wondered how Arthur, being a fisherman, felt about it, but you couldn't have paid me enough money to ask him.

"How did you and your wife get started in the restaurant business?" asked Blythe, but the expected reply never came. As her chopsticks crushed through a wobbly slice of tofu, the two dissected pieces splashed helplessly back into the vinegar muck, and one of them launched itself down the front of her dress. Jocelyn immediately took Blythe's arm and ushered her into the powder room. Before they left, Arthur whispered something to Jocelyn, and she responded with a nod.

"Paulie, we're going to plan B," he said. "Come with me." I followed him into a gleaming stainless steel kitchen, where four extra large pizzas sat under a row of heat lamps. He was pleased at seeing my grin. "Well, are you just going to stand there?" he asked, proceeding to laugh at his own joke and reach for two litre size bottles of Coke from the refrigerator. "Let's take these into the living room and get comfortable. Paulie, you take the pizzas and some paper plates." As I exited the kitchen, I couldn't remember feeling as buoyant in my whole life as I did at that moment.

Later, after we'd stuffed ourselves with "Sal's Award Winning Pizza" procured from a small family operation nearby, the four of us chatted amiably, enjoying each other's company and watching some T.V. shows. Then Arthur and Jocelyn took us outside to see the view from their second story porch. We murmured for a while about the view, after which our hosts discreetly exited, giving Blythe and I a few moments of starry night to ourselves. I wondered aloud what they would have done with all that pizza had we not shown up. Blythe shrugged, put her hands on my shoulders, and pretended to dance to some soft music coming from inside. I put my fingers on the spot still weakly stained from where she spilled her tofu.

"Listen I... uh.... this night has been kinda weird..." I started to say, fumbling for words, but she put a finger up to my lips to silence them, and then planted a long, sudden kiss behind it. Her perfume invaded my senses. It didn't smell expensive like Ba Ling's, but warm and remarkable just the same when mixed with the scent of her skin.

Chapter 23

Blythe's aunt was a sharp-nosed, suspicious old crone, well suited to the task of guarding her and her little sister. She always peered through the blinds whenever I dropped Blythe off and spied on us through doorways when I came over to the house.

I had good memories of Blythe, but we only had about three dates together before her parents reconciled and moved the entire family to Connecticut. I saw very little of her after that, although our strange and wonderful evening with the Fongs has replayed itself over and over in my mind ever since. We wrote to each other for a while but eventually stopped. I sent an e-mail recently to an address thought to be hers but never got a reply.

Several months before the move, she had abandoned her dance company, citing a falling out with Jerrod. "He's seen the last of me," she uttered tersely, but when I saw them together one final time, they shook hands and embraced in what appeared to be a fond farewell. That night when I escorted Blythe up the gated pathway to her house, she gave me another lingering kiss, said she'd had a wonderful time, and waved goodbye before closing the door. Her aunt glared at Arthur through the blinds in the kitchen window. I felt pretty full of myself and in a dreamlike state as Arthur's Caddy whisked us back across town, depositing me at the storefront. I suppose my kids today would have said I was "Stylin'."

Before I got out, he shook my hand. "Paulie, I'm sorry about the mishaps tonight," he began. He started to explain the idea behind our eccentric Chinese buffet, but I interrupted.

"What are you talking about Arthur? We had a super time. We're both very grateful to you for inviting us."

He laughed. "Well, you have to admit it was different. Anyway, you and your delightful companion are welcome at our house anytime; we loved having you."

"Arthur, I can't thank you enough..." I began, but he waved the rest of my sentence away.

"At least you didn't have to spend the evening with that aunt of hers, or you could have had yourself a real adventure," he went on exaggeratedly, pretending to mop his brow, to which we both laughed. He looked at me earnestly. "Say, I would love to meet your mother and stepfather sometime. Mei and Harry is it? I've heard so much about them from your uncle."

"I think that might be arranged," I said guardedly, being careful not to commit myself or them.

"Good ol' Paulie," he said, slapping me on the back. "As discretionary as the rest of your family, eh?" I offered a sheepish smile in reply. "Listen, Paulie," he said, lowering his voice and pinching his lips nervously between thumb and index finger. "Um...About what Jocelyn said concerning your uncle...I know that's supposed to be a family secret, I have no idea what she could have been thinking."

"Don't worry about it," I answered quickly. "I'm sure Blythe's forgotten it already."

"I hope so," he said with a frown, then he lightened up a bit. "Hey, I hear you met Bishop Frye not too long ago. That must have been something, huh? He's a famous guy around here; some people would like to see him run for mayor. He and your uncle go way back."

"So I've heard, but we didn't have much to say to each other," I said, reaching for the door handle, clearly not up for a discussion about the bishop. The plain truth was that I found the bishop disgusting, and I was still a bit rankled by the way he acted around my mother.

"I guess you didn't know he...."Arthur began but then abruptly broke off the conversation. "Oh well, we'll talk about it sometime. Have a good night, Paulie," he said. "See you Monday, eh? And tell your uncle I love him." I nodded and got out. Arthur's Caddy roared away in a cloud of smoke.

Within a year, Jerrod had managed to alienate everyone in his dance company, proving himself to be more of a tyrant and an abusive bully than a leader or an organizer. The small group disbanded, went their separate ways, and we were never to be graced by their presence at the school again.

The Taichi school, for its part, was humming as summer approached. Word got out among the students that there might be another tournament, but the committees had yet to reach a decision on where it would be held. The location of my uncle's school was brought up and immediately turned down. "Too small," he said. He also said something to the effect that he was too old to be bothered giving a bunch of idiots the run of the place and having to listen to them shout at each other all day like maniacs.

The Chinatown Y.M.C.A. gym, the scene of our last troublesome presentation, was booked solid for three months. Another location would have to be chosen, and the committees decided on an indoor ice skating rink in New Jersey that had been drained of its ice and closed off to the public for the summer months.

Up to that point, I had not had much occasion to wander far past the boundaries of the city or anywhere close to the land "across the river," as my mother used to put it. New Jersey had developed a reputation among my family in those days as an area ruled by common hustlers, and they were not far wrong. If that had actually been a correct assessment, however, New York City already surpassed it long ago, the crime rate having almost tripled in my short lifetime spent there as a teenager.

In an unprecedentedly short sighted move, Kuo suddenly deputized his wife, Mrs. Liang, giving her complete charge of organizing and overseeing all students attending the tournament as well as giving her final say as to who would or wouldn't make the cut. Seemingly adding insult to injury, he also gave her the power to change or alter any program entries as she saw fit, almost as if he were washing his hands of the matter. Fa was incensed. "The *nerve* of the old man," he grumbled. "And then to have to put up with that narrow eyed bitch calling the shots...no thanks, it's not even worth it."

"Adversity makes you strong," I quoted uncle back at him with a military smile.

"Oh no you don't, Paulie, no you don't....not this time," he said frowning. I laughed.

After a lengthy, fearless, and heartfelt attempt, Ba Ling once again lost her battle with sobriety. One dreary, rainy afternoon an emaciated and considerably stoned Ba Ling showed up at the school, dripping wet, pleading tearfully with my uncle to allow her to use his name so she could officially enter the tournament tryouts. She had long ago been barred from teaching at the school. Eavesdropping on the conversation as carefully as I could without being seen, I watched him shake his head through the glass partition in his office, angrily sticking a calloused index finger inches from her face. Though I couldn't pick up on the whole conversation, I clearly heard Uncle say, "I told you this kind of thing was going to happen, didn't I?"

The conversation was short, frightening, spoken entirely in Mandarin, and ended with Ba Ling shouldering her backpack and running out of his office, sobbing.

I watched my uncle's office window ripple during the event and hoped he had not been too hard on her. I wasn't sure how Ba Ling's fragile state would support this type of emotional let down, and I was pretty sure things would sour between them from this point on. One thing I could have predicted was that the resolute Ba Ling would ensure some way of proving to her returning coach, Xiao Feng, that she was still a viable contender, with or without my uncle's help.

Not too far from the Shaolin temple, on a mountanside in Hubei, resides what many consider to be the Shaolin's counterpart, The Wudang Temple, home to legend, folklore, documented history, philosophy and religion, all part of a rich antiquated stew forming the basis of Chinese martial arts culture. Some say the martial arts practiced here dwarfed anything the Shaolin monks could come up with.

Masters of the internal Wudang systems were said to be able to walk straight up the sides of buildings, fly over rooftops with their feet barely touching the ground, or engage the enemy in branches of the highest trees. It was among these people that a wandering Daoist by the name of Chang San Feng was first supposed to have lived and invented the art of T'ai Chi Chuan.

Legend has it that Chang San Feng drew his inspiration from a dream he had one night, in which he observed the movements of a snake fighting with a crane.

Uncle knew of some of these things, and he also knew enough to separate fact from legend, but he was mostly reluctant to bring up any subjects he felt Western culture wasn't ready to assimilate. As Arthur Fong pointed out, Uncle Kuo was capable of many feats of internal strength that he was loathe to reveal, and if witnessed by accident, even more reluctant to share. These feats were the individual product of time and effort, where whole days were spent in standing meditation and practices impossible to fit into present day schedules.

There were parts of rural China where Kuo's name was held in fear and superstition, but when I brought this up to him, he unsurprisingly refused to talk about it. What this traditional brand of secrecy meant for the core group, Fire, Sally, Tree, Metal, Earth Mother, and even myself and Fa, is that after years of dedicated study, we had yet to skim the surface of what my uncle really had to teach us.

For him, beyond a certain boundary lay this void to which all students of American residence were stubbornly barred admission. Even Ba Ling, to whom he taught the Da Lu, was not made privy to this deeper fountain of knowledge. It's not as if he deliberately withheld information. Indeed, he usually gave us more than we could handle and then some. Yet when I tried to approach him concerning scenes I had personally witnessed such as snuffing out of candle flames at a distance or disappearing and reappearing in front of his enemies, he became terribly mute and withdrawn. He once told me some of his Chinese friends were very upset that he had been teaching American students. There was some sense among them that he had been giving away national secrets. I laughed heartily at this. "My uncle, the spy," I almost choked, but Uncle took these matters more seriously than I could have imagined, and one could see that he was deeply hurt by it.

Chapter 24

When I finally walked inside the old warehouse building, risers were being set up in the pit of the ice skating rink. The core group and some Chinese students were waiting for my uncle up in the bleachers. I hoped I would beat him to the punch and not be the last one to show up. After taking a couple of subway trains and a bus to get there, it had taken me half an hour to find the place. Just then, the bar handle of a side door creaked open and he came flying out a few steps ahead of me. *Damn*, I thought as I saw Fa sitting there, twiddling his thumbs, and smiling. I was certain to get a chewing out about being late. Uncle wheeled around when he caught sight of me and frowned.

"Where have you been?" he interrogated.

"Trying to find the place," I answered with a dose of righteous indignation. "Take it easy, Uncle." I used a facial expression to plead with him not to go into a tirade among the students.

"To keep even a small animal waiting is unforgiveable," he lectured. Then making a sweeping gesture with his hand across the student body, he continued. "See everyone you kept waiting today? I had to waste their time looking for you. Sit down."

I squirmed in next to Fa. I would be tortured from both sides, and I knew it, but it was better than nothing. I knew it wasn't over with Uncle; he would wait for a few days and then suddenly ask me to clean out the school's latrines. These were "drop everything and get to it" mandates, and if you failed to heed them in time, things could get unpleasant fast. Fa looked over at me as if he'd just enjoyed a particularly satisfying meal.

Another door creaked open and slammed shut behind Ba Ling who stood with her back facing it in a red pleated skirt. Unlike Fa, who hadn't been privy to the scene in my uncle's office, I was fully prepared for some kind of showdown and hoped it wouldn't embarrass the daylights out of us all. Uncle immediately excused himself and walked over to where she was standing. Some words were exchanged between them in clipped Chinese, after which I heard my uncle saying that she could attend the meeting but that she had to be quiet. He also made it clear he was in charge of scheduling participants for the tournament and that since she was being sponsored by the Beijing Wushu Academy, if she had a problem with of any scheduling decisions, she was free to make an appeal to the board of directors.

Ba Ling nodded humbly and took her seat next to the group of Chinese students without so much as a glance in our direction. "I don't think your girlfriend likes you anymore," sneered Fa, who at that moment seemed to be revelling in my discomfort. I grabbed a pressure point on his shoulder, a trick shown to me not by my uncle but one of the Chinese students and told him to shut up or else.

"Owwwwch!" he yelled noisily.

The students turned around, and finding no cause for alarm, gave us a collective "Shhhhhh!"

Uncle glared at me again. Fa gave me a dark look. "We have wasted enough time," Kuo announced. "Let's begin. Fire and Water, I believe you have some suggestions for us." Fire, whose real name was Jim Davis, was bouncing his baby boy on his knee, the one my brother and I had seen at the baptism a couple of years ago, and Water, or Sally Waterman, was now in reality Mrs. Sally Davis. They were still recognized by their nicknames Fire and Water, even after all this time, except by the new students who had to be filled in. Sally was addressed as Sally on occasion but Jim Davis was and always would be "Fire," partly due to his fearless reactions on the night of the subway incident, but mostly because of his flaming red hair which was beginning to thin at the top. Metal, Wood, and Earth Mother were still recognized almost exclusively by their nicknames.

This time, however, Wood, the solitary, introverted disciple of my uncle's who kept to himself and rarely spoke unless he was in my uncle's presence, rose first. But before he could begin his sentence, the same side door wrenched open and slammed shut a third time, interrupting him. "Can I help you?" My uncle's voice echoed across the bleachers. Fire's head rose, and his ears pricked up like a young faun sensing danger. He shot my uncle a wild look of recognition as two familiar shapes in their dungarees took a seat at the far end of the bleachers near the exits, staring intently at the group.

Fire handed his son over to his wife. "Excuse me," Uncle continued, taking a few long strides towards them with Fire and Metal closing in behind. "This is a private meeting, can I help you?" The two got up and reluctantly shuffled out, but Fire and my uncle immediately recognized them as the two troublemakers who, along with their gang of hoodlums, had threatened them in the subway. Kuo posted Fire and Metal by the exits to ensure privacy and as a precautionary measure, then continued on with the meeting.

"As you were saying, Mr. Tree." He waved his hand at Wood, indicating that he should start over, but as soon as Wood opened his mouth he was interrupted yet again by the door flinging open and ushering in a flushed and chortling Bishop Frye. Both Kuo and the bishop nearly fell down laughing when they caught site of each other. Uncle was wheezing so hard he had to steady himself on a railing. The old men locked in a fond embrace, immediately wanting to know what the other was doing there.

"The secretary out front told me you and the kids were having a meeting in here, Kuo; it's so good to see you." He had come down to buy a winter skating pass for his twelve year old daughter and asked the secretary if he could take a look around, a request to which the star struck secretary gushingly acquiesced.

The two men were so happy to see each other, they almost forgot about the meeting and Wood standing there with his mouth open. The large bishop had become something of a national celebrity ever since his mayoral campaign made its debut. There were mug shots of him in the papers, and he had appeared in dozens of news reels; even the reclusive Wood knew him on sight. Everyone in attendance was stunned. I elbowed Fa in the ribs. "Remember him?" I asked.

"Sure," he snapped back. "Whaddya think I am, stupid?" I shrugged as the two men regained their composure and my uncle once again addressed the group. He put his hands on the bishop's meaty shoulders and turned him around to face us.

"I see you all know my friend Bishop Frye," he said, beaming broadly.

The students all smiled back and applauded. "And now my friend, I must take my leave of you," Uncle continued. "For we have much business to discuss, and so far this morning, we have accomplished nothing." He then shook Bishop Frye's hand who waved goodbye and wished us well, saying that hoped he could find some spare time to attend the tournament.

"It would be great if I could bring my daughter to see all of you," he said. "She loves judo." Fa and I smiled at the innocent mistake and waved goodbye to him, but the remark stayed with me. A daughter who loved Judo. Hmmmm. I wondered if he would actually bring her or whether he only said it to appear interested.

Wood, relieved at finally being able to put a few sentences together without interruption, wanted us to think about a simultaneous display of Taichi's five major styles, each to be performed by five individuals at the end of the program. It was an idea he got from watching a karate class go through its slow and deliberate "Kata" training sessions with each student simultaneously performing a different exercise best suited to their individual purpose. He remembered coming away from it with a feeling of euphoria generated by the trancelike experience.

The five major styles of T'ai Chi Chuan are named Chen, Yang, Wu, Hao, and Sun respectively. The names are derived from the last names of their forbears. In some styles the interconnectedness between them is visually obvious; in others such as the Chen style for example, it is more elusive. Sun, the most recent style to date, developed by Sun Lu Tang, combines all the major styles with some other internal arts such as Bagua and Xingyi thrown in.

This idea met with enthusiastic approval, and my uncle nodded his head throughout Wood's entire speech. Sally took down the minutes of the meeting, a job generally reserved for Mrs. Liang who could not be present that day because she was involved in submitting budget proposals to the committees. Everyone was pretty much relieved that she hadn't shown up and felt the morning's meeting had gone more smoothly without her predictable objections being raised every few minutes anyway. There were other suggestions, including one from Metal who wanted to light the end of his spear for a fiery routine that uncle said he would take under advisement. He was also dying to strategically place some of his metal sculptures on the stage risers to which uncle additionally replied that he would have to think about it. Earth Mother, who had watched the shabby uniforms she had painstakingly crafted years ago begin to deteriorate, offered to outfit us anew with the stipulation that she wanted to make some of them in different colors.

"I think it'll make a nice contrast when the students go to perform their different styles," she chirped. Another fine suggestion. Everyone murmured their approval and Uncle continued to nod, even though the students who would be chosen to perform these routines hadn't been selected yet. The suggestions continued to flow with everyone voicing their preferences and opinions on the individual routines they wanted to perform. Metal and Fire once again rejoined the group to present their choices after assuring my uncle that the two men who'd shown up earlier were long gone and no further threat to anyone.

Fa and I once again opted for the straight sword and sabre forms respectively, although I had long since tired of Ba Ling's "Red Guard" approach to instruction and felt ill prepared. I made weak excuses for having missed over a month's worth of private lessons and deliberately made myself unavailable to take her phone calls whenever she rang to discuss it. One day, however, she confronted me in person at the school. It was another rainy afternoon, and once again she appeared wet, drawn, and haggard from the after effects of a recent drug and alcohol binge. Her hair was still long and beautiful when wet and smelled like the fragrant plum flower blossoms Mom strategically placed around the store.

"Where have you been?" she asked with annoyed frown. I knew there was no way around this, so my only option was to plunge ahead. At first I looked down at my shoes, muttering an apology and trying to look suitably dejected. Then I decided to tell her the truth which was that I had smelled alcohol on her breath during our training sessions and felt that, at least for now, she was unfit to teach me. In retrospect, with the benefit of maturity and hindsight, I probably could have chosen a more tactful response. She was floored. Her mouth fell open then she turned ashen with rage. "Get this, my friend," she said, her gorgeous face twisting into a tight jawed expression. "No one in this whole country is more qualified to teach you than I am at this precise moment."

"Whoa! Hold on...I didn't mean..." I tried to interrupt, putting up a hand to stop her, but it was futile. The dam had burst, and her feelings of rage and frustration washed over me.

"Do I need to remind you that I'm seventh ranked National Women's Wushu champion of China? Do you have any idea how much work it took for me to get that title? I don't need this crap from you, Paulie. I haven't had a drink in months. I'm only teaching you as a favour to your uncle because of what I owe him. Your performance in our last lesson was disgraceful; it was as if you hadn't been paying any attention at all this whole time."

She was far from finished, and I imagined I deserved at least some of this, but the truth was, for all her blustering, Ba Ling's skills were still light years away from masters of my uncle's ilk. Had he been there, he probably would have ordered me out of the room, taken her aside, and given her a good old fashioned Chinese reprimanding, the kind that left emotional scars. I figured it was just as well for both our sakes that he wasn't.

"Ba Ling, please..." I began again, trying to apologize, but she cut me off.

"If you want to give up now, *fine!*" she continued, blasting me. "But you're a long ways off from mastering the jian, buster. A *long* way. At this rate it's going to take you twice as long as any of my other students. I don't think your uncle will be too pleased to hear *that!*" Her eyes glared threateningly. She carried on like this for quite some time, and after a few half-hearted attempts to make her see things my way, I gave up in exasperation, hung my head, and took everything she had to throw at me.

There were moments during her outburst when I desperately wanted to make her aware that just the mere fact of my being nephew and understudy to a famous Chinese grandmaster like my uncle placed me head and shoulders above her regular students, even though Kuo admitted she was something special. I watched her storm out furiously and wondered if the damage I'd mindlessly inflicted was irreparable, or if we would ever be able to speak to each other again. At the moment, she sat coldly across the bleachers from us, hands folded in her lap, quiet and aloof. I watched a Chinese student try to engage her in conversation and continued watching as she returned his eager glance with a smile. *Perhaps she's more comfortable being around them now than a half breed New Yorker like myself who can't even decide what to do with the rest of his life,* I thought glumly.

The candour in my uncle's voice could still, with surprising regularity, shake me out of a daydream. "Well that's it then!" he called above the hovering murmur of students, slamming shut a folder full of notes. "Thank you all very much!" The meeting had gone off without further interruption, and everyone looked very pleased with themselves. Ba Ling hadn't uttered a word or put up her hand the entire time, but now as everyone rose to leave, Kuo motioned her to stay behind. He looked at her solemnly. "I will continue to oppose your participation in this tournament by all means available to me, do you understand?" he asked. She gave him a defiant smile, turned on her heel, and walked out.

Chapter 25

A week before we were scheduled to do a run through with our individual performances, I suddenly changed my mind about doing the sabre form. This was due in part to an unexpected outburst from Arthur Fong when I informed him I would be participating in the event. "Why not do the Kwan Dao routine!?" he fairly shouted. "My God man! What have you been studying all these weeks for?" He knitted his eyebrows together excitedly. "Few people have ever even seen it before in this country. It would be *outrageous!*" He was yelling now, barely able to contain his excitement. "But you have to promise me one thing," he said, gripping me by the shoulders and locking me in his gaze. "If you do decide to do it, I want to be there. No exceptions, Paulie, and I want good seats for me and Jocelyn."

"Of course," I muttered, clearing my throat nervously and realizing that I had just committed myself. Arthur could be very persuasive, and his excitement was contagious. He threw back his brown head and laughed, exposing a row of shiny white teeth.

"This is going to *be fantastic!*" he said, pacing about in his living room. "I can't wait till you tell your uncle." Then his expression quickly faded and he put his hand on my arm. "That is...if you decide to do it, of course." His face brightened back up again. "Will Xiao Feng be there?" he asked. I replied that he would. "Hah!" he yelled, slapping the corner of a table with his thick, Japanese hand.

Actually, the person I would need to confront with any changes was Mrs. Liang, since my uncle had left most of the final decisions about the performances up to her. I should have known I'd be up against a brick wall. "It's too late," she huffed, pulling away with a stack of memos flapping in her hand. "You and Fa are scheduled already, and you will be performing... .er. . .let's see.. ..... *broadsword,*" she exclaimed finally, moving her red index fingernail down a column of type to a precise spot on the page and squinting at it through her bifocals. She brought her bifocals back to rest on her neck and beamed with satisfaction. I shook my head in exasperation. This was a third attempt at trying to explain my position to her, but there seemed to be no getting through.

Help came in the unlikely form of Jimmy Chow, who overheard most of the conversation while sorting through some files in his office. "What's going on?" he asked, pretending to be curious. There was something about his demeanour and the twinkle in his eye that made me realise he was about to save the day.

"I was just telling Paulie..." Mrs. Liang began, but Jimmy interrupted her with a convincing display of phony exuberance.

"Isn't it wonderful, Mrs. Liang? Paulie is going to be performing the Kwan Dao routine at the tournament; I just spoke with his uncle," he lied, grinning and shaking my hand a bit over-enthusiastically. "Congratulations, Paul," he said, continuing to shake my hand warmly. "We're all very proud of you."

Mrs. Liang had the amazed look of a toddler whose favourite toy had just been snatched away. "Well I..." she started in again with a confused squeak, but Jimmy steadfastly refused to let her finish a sentence.

"Now don't you worry about a thing, madam," he said, putting an arm around her shoulder reassuringly. "I'll inform the committee and make all the necessary changes in the schedule."

"Well... if you don't mind going to the trouble..." she said hesitantly.

"No trouble at all, glad to do it," he replied, patting her on the back and walking her away. I had to turn and put my hand tightly over my mouth to keep from laughing. He flashed me an okay sign, and I mouthed the words "Thank you" back at him as they left.

Later, Jimmy laughed when he told me about how he approached uncle with the news that I wanted to switch to performing the Kwan Dao, presenting it to him if it were a done deal. He said he was surprised when the only reaction he received from my uncle was a single raised eyebrow followed by, "How did you get that one past my wife?"

I've caught myself at various times smiling in memory of that remark. The ability to come up with zingers like those was one of things I found most endearing about Kuo. His despised wife and almost constant companion, the indomitable Mrs. Liang, was absent as had become her habit by now. Jimmy made excuses for her, saying she was nursing a sick relative, but it was obvious she could no longer tolerate being around the students and began distancing herself more and more.

True to his word, Bishop Frye walked in the day of the tournament accompanied by the daughter he'd said had been interested in Judo. There she sat, "Judo Girl," a mere child, straight backed with straight, brown, shoulder length hair. Their seats were astonishingly close to the judges and other foreign dignitaries. In fact, the entire event was set up differently and more elaborately than the previous one had been. Unlike the last time, many of the participants' families were in attendance, and we all relished our chance to gawk at them. My mother, Mei, and stepfather, Harry Chen, were there, as were Arthur Fong and Jocelyn, occupying the best seats in the house as promised. Uncle had pulled out all the stops this time, extravagantly hiring two lighting technicians with coloured lights run by a mixing board and a sound engineer who came complete with a state of the art public address system.

After an interminable wait, the skating rink's house lights dimmed, and the murmur of the crowd slowly died down. An unlikely emcee, my seventy year old uncle, crossed the stage with a few youthful strides toward a podium and adjusted the microphone. The microphone groaned and squealed as he twisted it this way and that, trying to make himself comfortable with it. After an agonizing few seconds during which the microphone's protestations nearly succumbed to complete silence, uncle's voice began crackling an introduction.

"Good...crackle, crackle... evening and welcome distinguished guests..." he began. At that we filed onto the stage and stood in a row, lengthwise, facing the audience. "My name is Master Kuo Yun San, and these..." he said with a sweeping gesture of his left hand, "Are my students!" At that point the house was brought down by such a tumultuous roar of applause and choruses of whistles that it felt as if we were being blown backwards. "Judo Girl" was on her feet clapping, joined enthusiastically by her father, Bishop Frye, and everyone else. I had to admit, she was striking for such a young girl.

Uncle stepped back to the podium and collared the microphone with his fist. "But first, ladies and gentlemen....allow me to present, all the way from China... THE BEIJING WUSHU TEAM!" he hollered into the microphone so loudly it retaliated by drowning him out in squealing feedback.

The Beijing team obligingly spilled on to the risers in their yellow satin shirts and their shaved heads. *More students windmilling themselves across the stage*, I thought. *More of the same.* I felt the pressure of the Kwan Dao's handle in my right hand and followed it down the gleaming axe head, the impressive halberd of General Ji Ji Guang. I silently prayed that his spirit would guide me tonight during my performance.

But the events were just beginning and there were plenty of other highlights to come, among them Ba Ling's much anticipated return to the competitive stage after a two year hiatus in the United States. Uncle, who had opposed her entering the tournament from the beginning, went outside to smoke a cigarette during her performance. As for Fa and I, wild horses couldn't have dragged us away.

"She looks stoned," sneered Fa as Ba Ling took the stage.

"Shut up," I warned, jabbing at his arm. She was sweating a little onto her sallow cheeks, her colour was bad, and there was a faraway look in her eyes. Her long pony tail drifted all the way down the confining satin back of her uniform. As she stood frozen in place with one sword held high up over her head, waiting for the music, to start; you could have heard a pin drop in the audience. Fa and I watched with a kind of morbid curiosity in stunned silence, hoping she wouldn't embarrass herself. Rumour had it that she kowtowed for days in front of pictures of Xiao Feng's ancestors, swearing that she was clean, and that he forced her to purge herself with a diet of raw vegetable juice for over a month before he would even consider letting her participate.

We all needn't have worried. Ba Ling was the success story of the evening. She performed her precarious double sword routine with such jaw dropping intensity that it prompted members of the Beijing Wushu Team to gape at each other in amazement. I was sorry Uncle missed her performance, but wrote it off to his usual stubbornness. I wondered how many of life's unique moments he had missed out on as a result of practicing this unyielding, typically self righteous behaviour. Probably plenty, but I also knew this to be one of the many unchangeable factors in his character that everyone simply took for granted. It was just him being himself.

As Uncle took the stage again and began fiddling with the microphone switch, we noticed shadowy figures in the background rolling huge metal objects into place with hand trucks. The houselights suddenly dimmed, and the stage was plunged into darkness except for a few towering metal objects which were lit from below with blue theatre lights. A man, naked from the waist up except for a red bandanna around his head, jumped out from the back of the stage and began banging out a loud, incessant rhythm on a dusty, old, Japanese "Taico" drum.

It was Fire. Those of us who recognized him fought to suppress a smile. The combination of his flaming red hair and red bandanna with the oil he'd rubbed on his body to make it look slick had Fa almost doubled over in agony from laughter. Metal entered from the left side of the stage, bathed in a white spotlight, replete with welding mask and spiked wrist bracelets. He had been working out prior to the performance, and his muscles were huge. Wearing only a white t-shirt and black martial arts style pants, he actually looked cool performing his

"Twin Mellon Hammers" form, so named for the shape of their enormous hammerheads. Fire had a pretty good rhythm going, and some of the audience was clapping to his drum beat. When Metal finished his routine, there was a thunderous, if amply prejudiced, applause. As I glanced out from the wings towards the audience, I noticed appreciative looks from all the females in attendance. Metal's performance had won them over, including "Judo Girl," who sat with her face transfixed, completely taken in by the spectacle. I was next. I stood waiting in the wings for the applause to die down, trembling in fear.

Chapter 26

I heard a crackle of static as Uncle began his next introduction. "And now everyone, we have something unusual and very different to present to you this evening..." I gripped the Kwan Dao tighter in my hands, the weapon which had been donated to the cause by none other than Arthur Fong from his private collection. When I arrived earlier that day at the skating rink, everyone was busy warming up and stretching for their routines. I made my way to a makeshift area backstage, set up behind some curtains, where we were supposed to make our entrances.

The Kwan Dao came packed in its own custom-fit weapons case which I placed on a folding metal card table, gleefully undoing the tiny gold clasps with my thumbs. The formidable weapon, resting in its long, black, velvet lined case, was always a pleasure to look at. Its overall length was eighty two inches, and it weighed about eight and a half pounds. The chrome finished steel blade extended some twenty four inches out from the end of the pole and was supported by beautifully cast, solid gold, dragon head fittings. I removed it from its case, feeling it for its balance and weight as I had seen my uncle do hundreds of times with various weapons.

The Kwan Dao's fit was unsettlingly perfect as if it had been custom made just for me. Even more unsettling was the bizarre legend surrounding it and the mysterious circumstances under which it came to be in Arthur's possession. Arthur took effusive delight in retelling the bone chilling story which I had by now heard several times.

Evidently, the ornate weapon once belonged to a Chinese nobleman who had a reputation for being unfaithful to his wife. In a fit of jealous rage one night, his wife picked up the weapon, attempting to sever the nobleman from his genitals while he slept. She was only partially successful, cutting off the tip of his penis. The reattached penis proved to be so horribly deformed that for the rest of his life, women refused to have sex with him, and he proclaimed the weapon cursed. One day Arthur received an invitation to a banquet at this same nobleman's house. Fong turned out to be the only Japanese man in a room full of Chinese and Manchurian dignitaries; he said he could feel the hatred in the room.

At least that was until his host appeared, presenting him with the Kwan Dao as a gift after discreetly informing his guests that the weapon was cursed and that no one would be more deserving of it than this Japanese dog.

When Arthur heard about the curse and what had been done to him years later, he laughed it off. "His curse was my good fortune," he said, beaming broadly, and proclaimed the weapon to be one of the finest specimens of its kind ever made, perfectly tailored to fit the smaller man or junior student. Knowing Arthur's propensity for exaggeration, however, I can only speculate that his so called legend was more than likely a product of his warped sense of humour. When I repeated the story to my uncle, he shook his head in disgust.

"The man is a big liar," he sputtered. "Pay no attention to this, Paulie; it's just another one of his crazy stories. I'm very disappointed in him that he would tell you such a thing."

"I now present to you," Uncle boomed into the microphone, finishing his speech. "Paul Chen, performing the Shaolin Kwan Dao form!" Applause erupted for ten seconds.

Distracted as usual, I had failed to hear the first few strains of music I'd chosen for the background of my routine and had to make a run for it. I ran past some girls from the Beijing Wushu Team who giggled at my approach and Jimmy Chow who gave me two thumbs up along the way. Mad at myself for not paying attention, I bolted on stage, got into a quick stationary pose, and paused before my routine.

I could feel the eyes of relatives and fellow students boring into me, ramping up my anxiety. When I looked out into the audience, I saw nothing but a black abyss, although the seating chart was affixed to my brain, and I knew everyone's location by heart. I began to sweat, and the pole felt slippery in my hands. Slowly as my eyes grew accustomed to the darkness, some familiar faces came into view. Xiao Feng sat front and center with his arms folded, along with a rather grim looking panel of judges from several Karate and Judo schools. Some I recognized from brief associations with my uncle, but the rest I'd never seen before. They all seemed to be wearing identical grey suits. Directly behind them, elevated and slightly to the left, sat Bishop Frye with his daughter "Judo Girl" who held a strong grip on my attention for the remainder of the event. It was almost impossible to take my eyes off her every move. She was suitably animated, now clapping, now smiling, and now talking with her father. Two rows behind them, further to the left, sat Arthur and Jocelyn. Arthur was straining forward, eyes glistening excitedly. Jocelyn's hand rested on his knee as if she were trying to hold him back. Occasionally, he glanced over in Xiao Feng's direction as if he were trying to capture some reaction from the venerable head instructor. But Xiao Feng, as if acting in defiance, sat solemnly poker faced and immobilized through the entire routine.

My mother and stepfather were sitting almost completely obscured, high up in the bleachers. Harry Chen preferred this discreet vantage point so he could avoid the dreaded task of mingling with the other attendees. Martial artists in China at that time were still considered inferior to men of learning such as my stepfather, and although my mother would have preferred choicer seats, he somehow managed to convince her that the location he chose would be more "suitable." His folded, milky white hands were all that was visible up the gloom.

Suddenly, the pole of the Kwan Dao slipped out of my grasp and I caught it in mid air just as it was about to hit the ground. I looked around terrified for a few seconds but no one even seemed to take notice. Encouraged, I managed to stumble through the routine, though I'd never in my life felt so sharply frightened or ill at ease. My hands trembled when it was over.

Afterward, Uncle said I caught the weapon with such lightening speed everyone could plainly see I was no novice, but I had my doubts. I felt the judges would surely penalize me for the gaffe, but my scores, although not great, turned out better than expected. When I returned backstage, I found Kuo methodically buttoning up his uniform and mentally preparing himself to give a demonstration with some of the advanced students. I stood there for a time, watching him smoothly going over a number of familiar T'ai Chi postures. When he saw me, he immediately stopped what he was doing and ran over to shake my hand, smiling warmly and patting me vigorously on the back. "Now that was some show, Paulie!" he chortled enthusiastically. I was less than exuberant about the performance and told him I felt I had made more than my fair share of gaffes. "Nonsense!" he bellowed with as much encouragement as he could muster. "Did you see their faces?"

"I saw Xiao Feng's face," I offered somewhat dejectedly. "He sat there like one of Arthur's jade statues. I didn't even see him applaud."

"That's just his way," replied Uncle, "don't worry about him, and anyway I heard he praised your performance and criticized Ba Ling for hers." He was almost mirthful. Then he grabbed my shoulders in his customary manner. "Listen to me," he whispered emotionally in an old peasant dialect I could never understand properly. "No one in this country has even seen this routine before, you should be very proud of yourself tonight for pulling it off. *I'm* very proud of you." He put his arms around me and gave me a big hug. Basking in his warm embrace did nothing to improve my defeatist mood. As usual, my inattention had led me astray, and I felt disgusted about having almost dropped the weapon. I shuddered at the prospect of making eye contact with Arthur and resolved to pack up and slip out of there as early as possible.

Now it was Fa's turn. "Show off!" Fa hissed jokingly out of the corner of his mouth as he ran past me toward the stage. Uncle laughed.

"See?" he said, gesturing with his hands outward as if to say, "What were you so worried about?"

Fa's performance was the exact opposite of mine. Poised and confident, he sailed through his wushu sword routine, dazzling the audience with speed and precision. My moodiness started to climb back behind the wheel. I glanced over at Uncle whose proud gaze took on an almost translucent quality. Fa's sword flashed and vibrated as he brought it behind his back to closing position. I should have been feeling nothing but admiration for my little brother who achieved his excellent standing due to hard work. Instead, when I saw "Judo Girl" on her feet, smiling and clapping for him, I felt an unwelcome twinge of envy. Instantly ashamed at myself for the thought, I was determined to make an exit as soon as the opportunity presented itself. If I could somehow manage to squeeze out of there unseen, so much the better.

Two events still mandated my appearance before scheduled teams began full contact sparring. A sizeable portion of the audience had come expressly to see some blood drawn and weren't about to leave disappointed. I thanked myself at the time for wisely choosing to be involved only with the demonstrations. With Fa, it had been a different matter. He deliberately asked to be pitted against some of the younger high ranking members of the Beijing Wushu Team. I praised him for his folly, knowing his skills would be severely outmatched by the Chinese team, but I still wanted him to know how much I respected his courageous decision. After all, his opponents had been bred for this type of thing literally since they were babies. I struggled with mixed feelings of guilt for not wanting to stick around and see my brother through this impending disaster, but in a way, I knew it was for the best. I just wanted to get home to my small bedroom at the dry goods store, draw the curtains, and hide for the rest of the weekend, ideally without having to talk to anyone. Before I could allow myself that luxury, however, there was a push hands demonstration to come with my Uncle and the much anticipated five Taichi styles demonstration of which I was a major participant. Instead of congratulating myself for having gotten through the Kwan Dao form and relaxing to enjoy the rest of the tournament, I silently cursed the fact that I had enlisted these two final obligations. There was nothing for it, I would have to soldier on, but at least the demonstration with my Uncle wouldn't take much time. All I had to do was let myself be thrown around the stage for a few minutes. What could go wrong? I felt a hand on my shoulder. "Ready Paulie? You seem far away."

"I'm ready, Uncle," I said, straightening in my uniform.

"Let's go."

Chapter 27

To my great relief, everything went smoothly as silk with Kuo taking control like a circus ringmaster. He gave me obvious cues so that I could time my falls without losing my balance. I couldn't help noting this was one of those rare occasions on which I would be facing him down in uniform. Kuo usually wore a raggedy t-shirt and an old pair of pants, even when he taught class. The moment was not lost on me. I felt an overwhelming sense of pride that here we both were, two family generations, facing each other in our crisp uniforms and giving a demonstration of an art we'd known since we were kids. We put on a good show for the audience who gasped in all the right places. Out of the corner of my eye I happened to catch the only change of expression I'd seen from Coach Xiao Feng the entire evening, a slight twitch below one eyebrow. It happened as Uncle made light contact with my wrists, after which I was instantly overturned and spun around backwards on my rear end. Xiao Feng covered one side his mouth and muttered something indecipherable to one of the other judges whose reaction was surprise. *Well, that's Uncle Kuo,* I thought, *full of surprises.*

Suddenly and unexpectedly, the push came, and it felt like I was floating backwards on an electric current projecting from uncle Kuo's forearms. Two other arms reached out stiffly to catch me as I was hurled offstage. It was Jimmy Chow, supporting my shoulders and looking down with a satisfied grin. The audience roared. I acknowledged them with a wave of my hand and bolted off the stage. *Just one more hurdle,* I thought, *and I'll be free.* At that moment, I realized I had just time enough time to attend to one last piece of unfinished business and hoped it wouldn't be too late. I charged with tennis shoes squeaking up two flights of rubber stairs, but froze with both hands on the railing when I got to the top.

There she stood, one stiletto heeled boot propped against the wall, silhouette framed inside the metal exit doors with rows of snowy pines forming a backdrop. Sunlight glinted through a small tear running down her cheek. By now I knew Ba Ling had heard Xiao Feng's sentence, and it hadn't been good. I also knew it was too late to comfort her, but I didn't want to get in the way of the moment so I just stood there. After a while, she looked up. Come to gloat Paulie?" she choked through a sob.

"Come to worship, you mean." I countered. "You were great out there, seriously." I finished a bit lamely with, "My uncle's an asshole sometimes, and Xiao Feng is a fat bag of wind. They say even his teaching days are over." She managed a grim, teary smile, pulling a tissue and a pack of cigarettes out of her knapsack. I struck a match from an old pack that had been languishing in my pocket for a week and lit her cigarette, grateful that they'd been there.

"He was my last hope." She sighed through an exhale. "I've got nothing now."

"Xiao Feng?!" I almost shouted. "You've got to be kidding. You're one of the best martial artists I've ever seen. Even Uncle thinks you're great. You can get a job teaching anywhere."

She smiled through a wet face. "Don't you get it Paulie? This was my last year to compete nationally for the Olympics. No one's going to take a chance on me now."

"That's crazy talk!" I protested. "I'm sure Uncle..." I started in, but she cut me off.

"Forget it, Paulie. I'm just too old now." I stared incredulously at a girl who could have passed for my slightly older sister. Were it not for the mascara running over her puffy eyelids, she would have looked like a teenager instead of the mere twenty-two year old she was.

But ravages of time had taken another toll on Ba Ling, weakening her fragile self-esteem. She had become distant and unresponsive, especially, it seemed, toward those who cared about her most. Few traces remained of the energetic beauty I once knew who greeted everyone with a smile and comforted friends in need. Now it was she who needed comforting and reassurance with a high maintenance level, but few were willing to get involved. Friends kept her at arm's length, frightened by her violent mood swings. To her credit, she attended a twelve step program, maintaining her sobriety for nearly a year, but it left her wary and bitter. She was plagued by substandard living conditions and continually worried over prospects for the future.

I started to open my mouth again, but we found ourselves listening to a distant voice calling from the downstairs hallway. Ba Ling suddenly grabbed my shirt sleeve. "Paul, aren't you supposed to be in the five styles demonstration?" she asked with an alarmed expression. I had almost completely forgotten. The voice called again and this time there was no mistaking the sound of my name. It was Earth Mother.

"I have to go," I said. "Listen; don't be so hard on yourself all the time. Things will work out; they always do." She threw me a glance that said I was getting dangerously close to patronizing territory. I took her gently by the arm and sat her down next to me on a ledge jutting out from the skating rink's unevenly plastered wall. It was an obvious attempt at a planter, except that it contained no plants. I could feel the heat radiating off of Ba Ling's newly acquired Calvin Klein jeans.

"Look," I said, trying my best to comfort her. "My uncle said you had 'greatness' within you. He sure doesn't say that about a lot of people." She grinned and gave me a side hug which felt sisterly.

"I can always count on you to make me feel better, Paulie." she moaned, putting her head on my shoulder. I wanted it to stay there forever. "You're my only friend." her voice murmured, trailing off.

I laughed at the absurdity of that statement. She had friends and more male suitors than anyone I'd known up to that point. "That's crazy talk again," I said, straightening up a little out of her grasp. I knew it would be best to retain a fragment of dignity and not be completely taken in by her charm.

"Paulie!" This time it was my Uncle's voice strong and with just a touch of rage.

As I got up to leave Ba Ling, she put her face up close to mine and whispered urgently. "Paulie, listen I may not be around too much longer and..."

"PAULIE!" The voice turned into an angry shout.

"And...I may be going to Europe. I've been invited by someone," she finished almost inaudibly.

"I have to go," I said again brushing my lips hastily across her cheek and sprinting toward my uncle's voice.

I turned just in time to catch her figure receding down a wet path. Tiny snow dots whirled in behind her, evaporating instantly as they made contact with the ground. It would be long time before we would see or speak to each other again. I do remember a prescient feeling of emptiness at that time, as though a piece of myself had suddenly broken off and gone missing. It was as if she picked that precise moment to vanish off the face of the earth.

Ba Ling moved to Europe permanently and unassumingly, taking up residence with a foreign exchange student in Amsterdam. A job cleaning filthy apartments served to keep her barely alive, but when the sound and fury of Bruce Lee movies reached European shores, she became much sought after as a teacher. Years later, while still in her twenties, she opened a successful chain of martial arts academies overseas and published two books about her life. One of them made it on to a European best sellers list. For now, I already missed her, and it would be a good many years before I came across her book while studying to be a journalist. I instantly recognized her picture on the flap and burst uncontrollably into tears, standing alone in the middle of a bookstore.

Suddenly disoriented from having run into Ba Ling, I started in the wrong direction up the stairs instead of down and almost plunged headlong into a pair of cotton twill pants finished off by patent leather shoes. Looking up, I saw Bishop Frye firmly holding his daughter's hand and staring down at me with a puzzled expression.

"Whoa! Paul Chen isn't it?" He continued to look bemused. "Where are you going in such a hurry young man?"

"M-my uncle..." I stammered.

"Oh yes, they're looking all over for you." The bishop interrupted. "Something about a demonstration."

"Yes," I replied. "I'm extremely late I'm afraid, and..."

"Well, before you go," the bishop interrupted again. "I just wanted to tell you how much Constance and I enjoyed your performance." Judo girl was only a few inches away from me now. I stared into her light blue eyes. *Odd for a girl with tanned skin and Asian features to have green eyes and be named Constance,* I thought. All that disappeared from my mind once we were introduced. "Paul, this is my daughter, Constanza. Her mother named her Constanza, I have no idea why, but everyone just calls her Constance. She's taking martial arts classes you know. She has an orange belt in Judo and we're very proud of her." I knew it was one of the lower ranks in Japanese Judo, and I suddenly thought of a T.V. program I saw recently offering lessons in Japanese. The teacher's heavily accented female voice spoke in my head. "Mr. Tanaka is going to the market... Tanaka-shi wa, shijo ni okotte iru."

"Oh Papa," Constance began, pinching the bishop's arm.

"Hi Constanza!" I said sticking out my hand. She gave me a look that said "You think you're so cool." I gave her a wry smile in return, so far I things were going swimmingly.

"What grade are you in?" I asked.

"Eleventh," she returned with a sour look that prevented me from saying anything else. I thought she was probably lying, but the Bishop said nothing. After some thought I decided to forge ahead, I was one of the stars of the show after all.

"I'm a senior," I said. "I'll be graduating this summer." She didn't reply but shot back another look that said, "Whoopie for you."

What I didn't know at the time was that Constance was extremely smart. While still only fifteen and very young looking for her age, she was placed in an accelerated program at her school due to the high marks she received on her entrance exams. She had already made junior in high school, just one year behind me.

"Congratulations on your belt," I murmured, afraid to say anything else that might alienate her. Bishop Fry bent down unpleasantly close to my ear and whispered something that made me feel sick to my stomach. "What!?" I cried out so loudly Uncle Kuo heard me on his way upstairs.

"Ah, there you are!" he said panting. "Where have you been? You're always holding things up. Excuse us, Bishop, wonderful to see you and your daughter again. Thanks for coming, but Paulie and I must go." The bishop nodded and smiled.

"Paulie?" sneered Constance. I gave her a dirty look but she continued to look amused.

"Come on," Uncle said, urging me down the stairs with his hand on my back. I watched the bishop hold the door open in a respectful, gentlemanly fashion for his daughter as both walked out. *She likes me*, I thought immediately, which turned out to be true.

Once we were out of earshot, Uncle turned to me and asked if the bishop had said anything of a personal nature about Constance. Still in shock from the bishop's words, I told Uncle about his whisperings of an affair he had some time ago with mother, even hinting the girl and I were possibly related.

"I thought he might tell you something like this...old women's gossip," Uncle said, sighing, his tone gradually becoming serious. "But I once confronted your mother about it. She told me she had nothing to do with him, and I believe her. I have it from a reliable source that Frye adopted the girl when he was on a missionary tour in Thailand. I imagine entertaining fantasies like having an affair with your mother has done much for his ego, but spreading gossip like this is unforgiveable. I intend to have a talk with him eventually, but in the meantime,

Paulie, put these stories to rest. It almost certainly isn't true, and even if it were, it does no good to dwell on such things. Anyway she's a rather pretty girl no? Well? Don't you think so?" he coaxed, elbowing me in the ribs. The feeling was like that of being poked by a gnarled tree root. I gushed out a laugh.

As we got closer to the stage, a young Oriental student with greasy hair, acne, and glasses was just finishing up his introduction of Uncle Kuo. "And now here to demonstrate for you the five major styles of T'ai Chi Chuan performed together are Grandmaster Kuo Yun San, Masters Paul and Fa Chen and two of Grandmaster's advanced students from the Kuo Yun San School of T'ai Chi Chuan." Some light applause ensued. Soon the countdown to full contact sparring would begin, and you could feel anticipation building in the room. Sooner than that, I hoped, I would be home.

No one felt the slightest inclination to join Wood who started inexplicably warming up onstage by himself. *Marking his territory*, I thought. He was proud the five styles demonstration had been his idea, but his efforts to take credit became something of an embarrassment. *Bully for him*, I thought. I was above such glory seeking behaviour. It was all I could do to focus attention away from the neon exit sign, behind which I hoped solace and refuge would shield me from disturbing new revelations about my mother.

The crowd reacted with stony silence to Wood's nonsensical gyrations but exploded into a roar of delight the minute Uncle Kuo took the stage. Master's pale, raised hand caught the glare of the spotlight when he slowly and deliberately commenced the first movement of the Yang form. My brother and I fell in behind him with the Chen and Wu forms respectively. Wood and Fire followed suit behind us with the Wu Hao and Sun style Taichi forms, creating eerie shapes on the curtained backdrop, like shadows formed by a hand puppeteer dissolving one animal into another.

When it was over, Wood was rewarded for his innovation by the tumultuous applause of an audience on its feet. Even Kuo was surprised by the overwhelming reaction. He grabbed Wood by the elbow, brought him forward and they both bowed. Wood was grinning from ear to ear. *Uh oh*, I thought grimly, *we'll never hear the end of it.*

Looking up into the bleachers, I suddenly noticed Kuo was no longer standing with us but had managed to sneak out into the audience and join Arthur and Jocelyn for a sit down chat. It also dawned on me that Fa was next up in the sparring competition and Kuo wanted a front seat. I knew this was a proud moment for my uncle, seeing my brother engaged in his first full contact sparring match. I also knew that conditions were ripe for my escape, which turned out to be dicier than I had anticipated. I felt overwhelming guilt at the thought of leaving my brother on the eve of his first sparring contest, but when the spotlights dimmed, I scurried behind the curtains into the wings. My mind raced. What would happen if I was recognized? Fortunately, most of the contestants were on or near the stage, and I could hear some gladiatorial chanting going on in the background. A woman screamed loudly "FAAAAA!" She sounded like my mother. I hoped my mother and Harry wouldn't make a big fuss about my leaving without telling anyone. My conscience bothered me a bit, but I told myself it was no big deal. I'd tell them I was sick. I'd tell them anything.

Once backstage, I hurriedly stuffed my uniform into a gym bag, shouldered the Kwan Dao, which I'd carelessly left on a folding chair, and made a dash for one of the lower floor exit stairwells. I was held back midway there by a fat palm pressed against my chest with a serious looking Arthur Fong behind it. "Just a moment, Master Chen," said the frowning face, leaning on the word "master" with obvious sarcasm. "I see you've conveniently forgotten all of my instructions tonight." Then he broke into a huge grin, and I knew he was kidding. Jocelyn sidled up behind him, taking his arm and smiling. "Congratulations!" He boomed happily. "Nervous at the beginning, eh? Well, sometimes that's to be expected. Did you see Xiao Feng's face? It gave me goose bumps!" He sputtered gleefully. His expression faded. "Oh... um... uh...I suppose it was too dark for you to see..."

"I saw," I replied quickly, humouring him. Truthfully, I thought the venerable head of the Beijing Wushu Association's face would have cracked if it ever changed expression. I'd never seen anything look so consistently impassive with the exception of Arthur's small jade statuettes as I mentioned before to Uncle. The undisputable fact was that I could see him plain as day and he rarely seemed to be looking at anything. This had to be another one of Arthur Fong's fanciful notions Uncle regularly accused him of. I breathed in Arthur's flattery with a sigh of relief, but I knew when it came to deciphering the mercurial mind of Xiao Feng, we were both out of our league.

"I trust you are taking utmost care of my gift?" Fong noted, pointing at the Kwan Dao.

"With what?" I replied absentmindedly, catching myself. "Oh...of course, of course, Master Fong. Thank you; I'm humbled by your trust." That seemed to satisfy him, and we shook hands. I said goodbye to Jocelyn.

"Be sure to return it when you come by tomorrow afternoon. My wife will have prepared tea and cake for a little celebration," he called out, hugging Jocelyn as I was leaving. I nodded and strode away at a fast clip, trying not to look too obvious, but when I reached the stairs, I took them whole flights at a time.

Following two bus rides, a subway trip and brisk walk into Chinatown, I was actually standing inside the threshold of my mother's dry goods store, letting the familiar grain scents and spicy aromas pour into me. I'd had finally made it home with few incidents, and I was dog tired.

Chapter 28

Uncle coined a saying from the old days he maintained was Chinese but could have just as easily originated in half a dozen other countries. It went something like this: "If you wait long enough by the river, you will see the body of your enemy float past you."

I knew Uncle and some others would voice their disgust over my untimely departure, but I didn't care. Of deeper concern was Fa, even though, as I predicted, he would understand. Besides, I learned later that he made a good showing, coming away with barely a scratch. There was also a moment after the Arthur and Jocelyn encounter which placed me at a scene I believe I was meant to witness.

Crossing a perilous stretch of highway outside the skating rink, I watched a man being cuffed by a gargantuan police officer and ushered into the rear of a squad car. The man glanced over his shoulder at me and a fleeting look of recognition crossed his face. His accomplice eyed me out of the rear window from a cage behind the front seat. The squad car then jerked away from the curb followed by two unmarked police vehicles. I gave a giant war whoop for joy in the middle of the street despite incredulous looks from fellow pedestrians. I'd recognized the two men instantly as the ones that had been dogging my uncle and threatening him in public this whole time. I was also provided with a good enough story to throw any hounds off the scent who might be inquisitive as to my whereabouts, at least temporarily. I was ecstatic.

I slid the heavy Kwan Dao case, which I had been carrying this whole time, off my shoulders, discovering that sweat had attached it to my jacket. In the distance, I saw a folded note perched on my mother's store counter. I held up one crimped end of the note with ragged edges to the light without knowing what I was looking for. Perhaps a childish quest for invisible ink. It was a note from one of my mother's customers.

"Dear Mei Chen," It read in Chinese characters. "Thank you so much for the sample of tea and extra pound bag of rice. We are grateful." In that instant, everything was back to normal. I was home. I flew upstairs to my room, flopped down on the bed, and pulled a comforter over my face. The next day was a rainy Sunday, most of which I slept through, thankfully without being bothered.

In the following weeks, it became impossible not to dwell on Constance and our strange but exciting encounter. I shuddered at the spectre of my mother having an affair with the bishop, but I decided to approach her carefully on the subject. At first I thought perhaps I'd set a trap and see if she fell into it into it, but decided the wisest course would be just to come clean, tell her what I knew, and see what she had to say.

"Where did you hear that, Paulie?" she asked quickly with a worried frown. This wasn't the reaction I hoped for. I wanted a quick denial followed by some anger at the intrusion into her personal life. When I finally told her the truth, she said to my unbounded relief that she'd heard a few rumours and that she had never had an affair with the bishop nor would ever consider it. A judge would have let her off for the flawless performance that followed. "These are silly stories, Paul, jokes told by silly old men to puff themselves up. His daughter is adopted, a tiny Vietnamese missionary girl as I recall, who some say bears a resemblance to me and whose father was too poor to take care of her. Remember, I have always told you the truth." She had. I remembered. I fully believed her now, and nothing in the world could shatter that belief. Right then, I felt like hitting the old bishop in the mouth for telling his lies about my mother and our relationship would be forever strained. Oddly enough, my relationship with his daughter, Constance, flourished. Still testing, I asked mother if she'd ever heard the name "Constance."

"No, Paulie, would Constance be a new girlfriend?" I never thought of it that way, but now that she mentioned it... I could never have imagined being up to my knees in a shag rug at Dartmouth College proposing to her after only a few months into our relationship.

Sometime prior to our dating period, I'd come across a write-up in the paper about a Judo tournament at a local school near the theatre district. Four names stood out in bold typeface; one of them said Constance Frye. I ended up talking Jimmy into driving me part of the way, but cringed when I saw the state of his wrecked car, smoking like an ashtray. I fibbed to him that someone was giving me a lift home and told him that he should really look into getting some new wheels one of these days, but he laughed it off.

Entering the Judo school for the first time, I was assaulted by a powerful odour of stale, sweaty feet. The place was a disaster. Tracks of dust on the floors, Styrofoam cups and cans of soda spilled onto shattered table tops. Most of the chairs had been demolished, but sat there like wounded veterans awaiting a final execution. Uncle always kept his studio obsessively tidy, periodically throwing open windows in the dead of winter and burning incense to quash the odours. Some of his students behaved like servile monks, sweeping the floors and cleaning the toilets. I remember being horrified when I witnessed the conditions of this place and wondered how the students could stand it. Gradually, once the foul smell wore off, I became used to my surroundings, figuring the sheer numbers of students attending these classes would probably be difficult to control. I put a lid on my reactions, pretending to be as still as possible so as to blend in with the rest of the onlookers until the right moment. I didn't have to wait long.

Fifty students emptied into the room from two side doors as if they were squeezed out of a tube. They stood in formation like rows of dominos until a portly man entered in a rumpled Judo uniform, or "Gi," as they were called, and barked a command in Japanese. The students responded instantly, seating themselves cross legged in a circle around the room facing what I supposed to be their teacher. Suddenly the onlookers became quiet. The man in the rumpled Gi pointed out two students who immediately sprang to their feet, bowing to their teacher in a manner I had not seen before. One of the students was a swarthy, fit young man, not much older than me, who obviously looked as if he'd been working out. His chest and arm muscles protruded through his shirt, and some of the female students seemed quite enamoured of him, clapping and shouting out his name when he got up to take position. His opponent was a thin, fragile looking girl I estimated to be no more than fifteen, with pale, Asian features. They bowed to each other again and locked arms Judo style, but the girl was too fast and had the jump on her adversary before he could control his footing. She flipped him, banging his head so violently against the floor that the sound echoed across the ceiling. I let out an involuntary laugh, clapping enthusiastically along with everyone else. The young girl turned and smiled. It was definitely Constance. Trying to hide a pained expression, the boy scrambled back into position and attempted to regain his composure. The teacher watched them both like a Cheshire cat at a tennis match, crossed legged and stone faced. The teacher then called out two other students. The boy seemed dumbfounded, like he'd just been wounded. Constance reclaimed her seat.

I was glad for the opportunity to see Constance in action this early in the proceedings and debated whether I should attempt to say hello or slip away unnoticed. Before I could decide, I looked up to find her staring down at me.

"Well...Paul Chen...this *is* an honour." She said it in a tone that made me wonder if she was being sarcastic. Feeling unsettled and somewhat embarrassed, I got up to shake her hand.

"The honour's mine," I said, attempting to look as indifferent as possible. I lied to her that I was on a mission to compare Chinese wrestling, or "Shuai Chiao," to Judo at the suggestion of friends who insisted I see the tournament, but I knew she wasn't buying it.

"You have *friends*?" she asked, looking playfully surprised. "And to think you came all this way...this really is a tremendous honour for me," she continued unabated. She had been sitting next to me, and I'd been waiting patiently to reply when she suddenly stood up and stuck out her hand. "Well, I do hope you got your money's worth."

"Wait!" I found myself shouting. "You did great. I'd like to see you again." But she had already begun skipping down the bleacher steps. "Hey!" I was yelling this time. "When can I see you?"

"Dunno," she answered. "Gotta go."

So began an introduction to the endlessly frustrating, contradicting and mysterious ways of Constance Frye leading up to our marriage. Dartmouth College accepted our transcripts a month apart, and we married a week later. We married young, but luckily Constance is the anchor of my life, and at one time, the only thing holding it together. We have two children of whom I'm extremely proud and a rollercoaster marriage behind us that, in a strange way, always felt secure in. Our children are both boys and, of course, budding martial artists. I keep telling them I'm still in the budding stage, continually borrowing maxims from my uncle who assured me with great regularity that it took two lifetimes to become a good martial artist.

Constance was a major participant in one more scenario, neutralizing two attackers while fully dressed in her school clothes. One attempted a stranglehold from behind while the other grabbed her shirt from in front. Both were again dispatched quickly in a well rehearsed manner that left Constance smiling again, amid much clapping and nodding from the audience. After some thought, I realized this had been enacted for promotional effect, a clever attempt to entice women into the school's self defence program. Soon after, Constance bowed curtly and left the floor.

I decided this would be my cue to leave. I'd made enough of an appearance, and the hot, vile odour of the place was taking its toll. When I got up to make my way through the aisle, a short, baby faced student ran up to me clutching a piece of crumpled notepaper.

"Constance said to give you this," he managed breathlessly, handing it over. There was nothing on it. "Hey!" I called after the kid as he ran away but when I turned the paper over I saw a big "C" and Constance's almost illegibly scrawled phone number on the back. My heart leaped for joy. It took me almost a week to figure out whether she'd written a four or a six, but I finally got it straight. My exit from the building was greeted by a warm dusty breeze, a foretelling of changes to come.

Chapter 29

Two events loomed that would forever alter the course of our lives that summer. The first would change the family's relationships in ways we couldn't possibly predict. The second would tear my uncle away from us for good. The first was a decidedly happy one for me. I was finally graduating from New York City's public school system and was duly elated. When I stepped on the platform to receive my diploma, a giddy sensation swept over me which I can summon up to this day. There would be college to think about next, but I promised myself a few months off to relax or to travel and see a foreign country. Some friends relentlessly tried persuading me to join them on a sightseeing trip to Switzerland. At first I declined, then I started to warm up to the idea, but when the time came, I still couldn't make up my mind, and they left without me. In the end it turned out to be just as well that I stayed put. Life changing circumstances were beginning to unfold that would inevitably set my course for the future, even though the future seemed a long way off.

Practically my entire family was in attendance on graduation day. Uncle shook my hand solemnly, and my teary eyed mother, Mei, embarrassed me in front of the congregation by throwing her arms around my shoulders and giving me a big kiss on the lips like she used to do when Fa and I were kids. Fa gave me a limp handshake while barely looking in my direction. Harry Chen grabbed me by the shoulders, sporting a yellow, toothy grin, shaking me back and forth like a rag doll. Everyone else, including Mrs. Liang, shook my hand and told me this was one of those days I would remember for the rest of my life. I wasn't feeling all that pleased with myself, but more relieved that it was over, and I was ready to start a new chapter in my life.

On a particularly humid day that summer, Uncle Kuo was sitting on his neighbour's porch, smoking a cigarette and whiling away the time. A mailman came by, handing him a letter with his address scrawled on the front, and a red wax seal with a bunch of Chinese characters printed on the back flap. The letter was also in Chinese characters, and it took uncle almost two hours to read it because he couldn't find his glasses. After re-reading the contents of the letter, smeared and smudged with red inked fingerprints a third time to make sure he hadn't missed anything, Kuo's eyes welled up with tears.

"My brother is dying in Taiwan," he announced to us solemnly after one of my mother's particularly satisfying family dinners. Mrs. Liang was there and remained silent, staring into her lap. The death of a family member is always a painful, tragic event, but especially with Chinese families, it becomes an exquisitely morbid affair, including superstitious deities and ritualistic ancestral worship. Mrs. Liang felt doubly sad this night for she had other unfortunate news to tell her husband, news which for the time being would have to remain secret. A tear rolled down my uncle's cheek and he let loose an emotional sob, wiping his glasses methodically with a stained handkerchief and making a concerted effort to retain his composure. He swallowed hard and continued. "They say he has been diagnosed with pancreatic cancer, refuses to leave his house, and there is no family member available to take care of him."

Mei held a hand up to her mouth as was her custom upon hearing news which either shocked or frightened her. My stepfather looked at him gravely. "Does this mean you will soon be leaving us, brother-in-law Kuo?" Now he had everyone's attention, especially mine and Fa's.

"Yes," Kuo replied. "As I said, there is no one there willing to look after him, and I must go immediately, as soon as my affairs are in order." We all knew he was serious. In keeping with Chinese tradition, loyalty to family members was paramount. The announcement was so sudden that everyone around the table gaped at him, with the exception of Mrs. Liang who continued to stare at the floor between her shoes. In fact, my mother had never met her other brother, Kuo's twin; someone who led the life of a virtual hermit managing the affairs of a Taiwanese monastery. She wouldn't have even had a glimpse of him were it not for an old photograph in very poor condition that Kuo had once shown her. I went over in my mind all the time and effort Kuo had spent committed to founding a school and practice in the States only to abandon it at the drop of a hat just because a brother with whom he almost never communicated was ill. Looking back, it made no sense whatsoever. As if all this weren't strange enough, it was common knowledge among family members that the two rarely got along. Whenever questioned about this mysterious twin brother, Kuo would only shake his head, grumble something unintelligible, and walk away looking upset. Making her unique contribution to the gloomy atmosphere that evening, my mother bit her lip and cried tears for a brother she would never know, living out his final weeks on earth. All Fa and I could think about was the prospect of Kuo leaving us for an undetermined stay in Taiwan from which he would possibly never return. Despite being offered a delicious dessert, we inexplicably lost our appetites.

Before Kuo left, however, he would be counted among the assembly attending my graduation, at which time I introduced him to my first and only serious love interest. I gave them a simple, no frills introduction.

"Uncle Kuo," I said. "This is Constance." To my profound embarrassment he began looking her up and down with a curious smile, giving her a thorough appraisal as if she were a piece of livestock. Finally, he nodded with a look of satisfaction. She was expressionless. I wanted to crawl underneath the lawn chairs.

"So you're the young lady we've been hearing so much about," he boomed, loud enough for everyone to hear. She looked at me and smiled, although at this point I could not have been more embarrassed. Constance had a funny way of appearing to enjoy moments that made me feel uncomfortable.

"Sifu, it is about you whom everyone talks," she returned boldly in her best Mandarin which, if a little shaky, was at least direct and to the point. Uncle was obviously flattered. I'd had it. I steered her politely away from my family by suggesting we get something to refresh ourselves and left Kuo standing there, beaming in his own pool of contentment. Soon after I was accepted at college, we would be married.

The core group, along with myself and brother Fa, gathered for a farewell party in Kuo's honour which was to include a final class from the master. Uncle's sombre mood was evident from the moment he showed up. He was, of course, crushed about having to leave us, and I saw more than one look of resignation cross his face amidst obvious attempts to appear pleased. But after some forced laughter at his bad jokes, a little good natured ribbing, and nostalgic reminiscences about the old days he brightened, at which point we noticed some of the old spark return.

Fire laughed about the early days when he remembered a Chinese translator who, having been recruited to help out, could make no sense either of Kuo's English or his Chinese and kept giving faulty instructions. He would often have half of the class going one way and the other half trying to catch up until they piled on top of each other in mass confusion. It was the first time I'd seen Kuo chuckle in weeks. Sally admitted there were times when she feared for her life during some of Kuo's park demonstrations, always unrehearsed, after which she arrived home and her mother would notice her hands trembling. There was a loud gasp and an explosion of joy from the entire assembly when Metal made a hulking appearance in the doorway. He had just returned from a show of his sculptures in Paris and couldn't stop talking about it. Kuo fixated on every word until he became distracted by a package making its way to him from across the room. With glistening eyes, Earth Mother presented him with a gift, a brand new fedora hat with almost the identical brim as his old one. It was made by Stetson, one of America's leading hat manufacturers. She hastened to mention that it was not made in China by the most beautiful women in town, but bestowed in reverence by a fat middle aged one who loved him very much. He thanked her, gave her a big hug, and almost cried himself, something we rarely saw.

Having drained couple of glasses of champagne, Kuo felt a renewed burst of vigour and led off the Yang long routine, still barking commands at us if he felt our body parts weren't moving together in perfect unison. It was a window in time that stayed with us long after his broken promise to return.

A scant few weeks before his departure, Mrs. Liang informed my uncle she had been seeing someone else, that she would not be departing with him for Taiwan, and that she wanted to be granted a divorce. Kuo flew into an uncharacteristic tirade. He furiously accused her of shaming him and his ancestors, reminded her of his unflinching devotion, then accidentally brought a fist down on the edge of his writing desk, breaking off one corner while its legs gave way beneath it. Mrs. Liang sat stoically through it all until Kuo realized any protestations or efforts to dissuade her would be futile. He made sure to convey to her, however, in no uncertain terms, that she was abandoning him at one of the most troublesome times of his life, and that she would soon come to regret it after all he'd done to nurture their relationship. He demanded to know who the other person was and enquired as to the depth of their relationship but was given no information in return. Finally, after having said little of consequence, Mrs. Liang got up, walked out the door of his apartment and out of his life for good. A year or so later, a Chinese official tracked him down while visiting some relatives in Sichuan Province and served him with divorce papers. He took a moment to read them while finishing a cigarette, then quickly signed and dispatched them back through a rural post office to New York City. It took so long for the papers to reach Mrs. Liang's sweaty, shaking hands that she collapsed from nervous exhaustion when they finally arrived and was bedridden for almost a week.

Following days of preparation in which Fa and I packed an endless series of backbreaking cardboard boxes, the time grew near when we would be bidding a final farewell to my uncle Kuo.

With disorganized, bustling, and tearful goodbyes, family and friends saw him off one docking station down from the one he'd originally arrived at almost five years earlier. Even the weather made itself into a carbon copy of that time, foggy and bleak. He waved to us from inside a black, rain slicked parka until he and his enormous, frighteningly ill maintained vessel disappeared through a bank of mist followed by the blast of a horn from a lonely tugboat.

The school, it was decided, would be left temporarily in the hands of myself, my brother and Jimmy on the condition that we made every effort to uphold its traditions while keeping it going as long as we could. The core group agreed to be on hand as much as possible to help train new students and continue guidance with the older ones.

As soon as word got out that he left, we immediately started losing money. I was rarely there, busy with college entrance exams. I left Fa in charge with yet another year left to graduate and Jimmy who was approaching retirement age. We had one final meeting in Kuo's old office with me presiding in his oversized leather desk chair. We would turn the property over to a Karate chain owned by a kickboxing champion and fledgling movie star who, unbeknownst to us, would turn out to be a box office smash. I remember we all breathed a sigh of relief at being out from under the school's increasing financial burdens, but two decades later, on a purely nostalgic impulse, I bought the building back from the foundering dojo along with the property it sat on. Uncle Kuo had probably been dead a long while by then, but I reasoned for some time that he would not be returning to attend my wedding as promised.

Chapter 30

In the end, my marriage ceremony tended to reflect the qualities of my future wife, small yet amazingly beautiful. Constance, being slightly dark skinned and a natural beauty, wasn't used to wearing much makeup, but I had to admit touches of it in the right places made her look radiant, especially the day she was presented to me. Once the veil of her classic wedding gown was removed, I was completely bowled over. I became speechless and nervous around her for one of the few times in my life. The bishop, her father, insisted on presiding over the ceremony and reading our vows in the Catholic tradition. We agreed to this, although Constance adamantly refused to have our wedding in his big cathedral. The church we picked out embraced us warmly and turned out to be just the right size for family and friends. Both our families pitched in to make sure the place was beautifully decorated with added ceremonial touches designed to represent both Taoist and Christian faiths. How they did it all, I'll never know, but everything meshed together perfectly and everyone couldn't have been more pleased, particularly me. I was about to be married and embark on a new life.

I felt proud and exhilarated beyond words and felt special electricity in the room when Fa handed me the ring. It was a solid gold hand-me-down my mother received from her mother, ornately engraved with tiny twin dragons on the inside for good luck and harmony. I discovered sometime later that my father-in-law, the tattle-tailing Bishop Frye, had a good side to him as well and helped my family out of several scrapes without letting them know about it. For now, his comments about my mother were still fresh in my mind even as I tried my utmost to be cordial around him. A reception was thrown for us at his lavish house on the beach in East Hampton, once home to screen legends of the thirties. Constance and her girlfriends baked us a delicious wedding cake which most of my relatives spat out in the rear garden, with the exception of Fa, who helped himself to a third piece.

People donated lots of beautiful flowers, and huge bouquets of exotic smelling orchids were everywhere along with giant candles lit for the occasion. Fa joked the place looked like a funeral parlour, but I saw it as a complete rebirth, an awakening to a new life.

Fa never married. To this day he still lives in Chinatown in a tiny room with his dog over a print shop that he has run singlehandedly and with fierce pride over the past thirty years. He still teaches and spars with friends on occasion. A true master of the "jian," he fenced with me recently, beating me so soundly that within a couple of minutes that I caved in and bought him a beer for his trouble. I secretly always thought Uncle favoured him over me, but when I brought it up one day he told me he always thought it was the other way around. I still loved Fa. He had me over a barrel once or twice with the family, but overall, as brothers go, he turned out to be a decent sort. Even as I later became financially successful with "Chen Enterprises" he never asked me for a penny, though I knew he had many times struggled to keep his fledgling printing business afloat.

When Kuo Yun San finally arrived in Taiwan after a brutal voyage, he searched for his ailing brother for a number of weeks without success. The first door he knocked on was the monastery where his brother worked, but as soon as he brought up the family name, he was refused entry. Finally, after several more rounds of furious knocking and door bell ringing, an abbot came out, carefully closing the door behind him, and beckoned Kuo into the courtyard. The abbot explained to Kuo that government officials were looking for his brother due to the fact that he contracted labourers for much needed repairs at the monastery but ran out of money to pay them. He went on to say that his family members were hiding him, moving him from place to place like an outlaw and that he had no idea of his whereabouts. Though his brother was by now gravely ill, he refused treatment for fear of being found out and running the risk of having family members bear the burden of debts they could ill afford themselves. Kuo cursed under his breath, waved goodbye to the abbot, and left, seething with anger at not having been told all the facts. After an exhaustive search, Kuo at last came upon relative who told him his brother was under the protection of a band of monks who kept him holed up in a small monastery on the outskirts on Taipei, close enough to the city to avoid suspicion yet far enough away to avoid detection, whereupon he was entrusted with a map and well wishes.

"Be careful," warned the relative, the monks were armed, dangerous and vigilant, having been trained in various forms of combat and guerrilla warfare. Kuo told the relative not to worry.

Neither myself nor Fa ever heard from my Uncle again. No letter. Not even a postcard, right up until his untimely death. My mother was the only one kept informed of his whereabouts through the occasional letter, and she warned us previously of his desire for his activities to remain henceforth secret from everyone in the family. When I relayed this conversation I'd had with mother to Fa, we both wondered how come our uncle was acting so strange and continued attempts for years to pry information about him from her, but she refused to budge. Thereafter, information reached us only in small, incomplete fragments until his death. Each fragmentary piece of news led us further into obscurity until we decided at some point that master Kuo's life would ultimately remain a mystery.

Fa surmised, after some time had passed and we still hadn't heard from him, that being a fiercely proud individual who insisted on having things done his way, somehow got himself entangled on the wrong side of local government. Kuo prided himself on being a law abiding person no matter what country he happened to be in, and it would have been typical of him not to want any family members to get wind of anything that could have been mistaken for impropriety.

In a state of anguish, he wrote my mother one final time. Although no evidence remains of the letter, we could only guess the substance of it dealt with the fact that he had unfinished business in Taiwan and that it was doubtful the family would ever see him again.

The old dance building where Kuo once ran his school is now the property of myself and Chen Enterprises Inc. It houses three of the firm's senior accountants for part of the day after which a night staff takes over, their faces lit by banks of terminals along with data processing machines that print most of our daily reports. I still get the same old feelings unlocking the front door with my key and running up the steps to that first set of double doors as I had dozens of times when we were kids. We seemed to be constantly running errands for an uncle we worshiped beyond words.

The studio is now used as storage space for stacks of paper in brown wrapping, indiscriminately and voraciously eaten by computers. Upon entering the room, one is always greeted by the loud skittering of cockroaches, scurrying to their hiding places whenever a human species makes his or her startling appearance. I smiled to think about how my uncle would react if he knew his former studio had been overrun by these creatures and how, in those days, he probably would have made me scrub everything from top bottom, sprinkling potions around to get rid of them.

Office girls generally appeal to their male counterparts when it comes to fetching paper out of this room during evening hours, but of course, I have very different memories of the place. Standing in the middle of that room, I heard not cockroaches but Ba Ling's musical voice, talking among a group of students. I could always pick her voice out of a crowd. Or memories would come back about watching her, in silence, change out of her slippers and begin the deliberate movements of her sword routine. With minimum effort, I could conjure up sounds of dance students' footsteps running down the hall, hoping class hadn't started without them. It was nights like this when I enjoyed being in this room alone late, listening to sounds only I could hear, particularly on a night which became something of a ritual for me over the years, Kuo's birthday.

The sound of squealing tyres and a breaking bottle outside snapped me back into consciousness. I glanced at my watch. I'd been standing in this dark room alone with a bottle of whisky for several hours, and my old habit of being lost in thought was creeping back. It was time to punch in the building's security code and start heading toward my office, if I missed my business partner this time, I could count on all hell breaking loose.

Some of the core group and I met occasionally at a few of Manhattan's many popular restaurants, renewing the pleasure of each other's company and reminiscing about the old days. Most moved to the suburbs or further out to different cities, so our meetings dwindled in size over the years. Whenever the subject of my uncle came up, however, the conversations turned more animated. 'When had I seen him last?' and 'What was he doing these days?' were the most frequently asked questions.

I could only shrug in response and tell them that the last we heard he'd joined up with a monastery in China. I was only being half facetious of course, but the statement usually garnered the desired reaction, even if those present had heard it a few times. I took a certain pleasure in throwing them off guard, but it was my turn to be surprised by a statement Wood made during one of our gatherings. Through a series of strange connections he had somehow also become the student of Arthur Fong for a period of time. I kept my mouth shut and let him finish. After he was done I was glad I hadn't opened it. He went on and on about this Japanese guy who lived in a house full of stuffed animal heads and about how eccentric he was.

"I studied with the Fong guy for a year until I was convinced he was out of his mind," Wood concluded. I tried to hide a smile behind my glass of water. I knew the value of Arthur's teaching well, just as I knew the value of all teachers. Later that evening, Wood took me aside and told me the Fongs spilled the beans to him about having received a last letter from my uncle after he told them he had been Kuo's student. Although he begged them to see it Arthur told him he'd long ago discarded it and would only say it was private, containing a few pleasantries and his signature.

"How about an address?" I asked anxiously.

"Sorry old man," came the reply. "The Fongs made it abundantly clear this was privileged information."

Not to me, I thought, and resolved to pay Arthur and Jocelyn a visit in the very near future.

Chapter 31

"Of course, my boy, come on over!" Arthur yelled so loudly over the telephone that I temporarily lost my hearing. Arthur's health had been declining steadily over the years, and I remember being shocked to see him when he greeted me at the front door in a wheelchair. In earlier times, he was one of the most robust men I'd ever seen. Jocelyn at sixty five was still ravishing and cool as a cucumber. She pushed Arthur to one side and bent forward to give me a peck on the cheek.

"All right you two lovebirds," grumbled Arthur, after which he was given a playful slap on the shoulder. "Come on woman," he ordered. "Take us into the sun room so we can talk." I had brought more than one girlfriend here over the years, but this wasn't a social visit, and I resolved to get as much information out of him about my uncle as I could.

Once again, we were served canned Cokes on a silver tray, but this time it was Jocelyn who brought them. Arthur took his time pouring his customary drop of rum into one of the cans from a half finished pint. I couldn't help but get straight to the subject I'd come about.

"Arthur," I asked him point blank. "What's this news about Kuo? I heard from a friend that you received a letter from him. The man hasn't written us in over two years. Where is he? What's happened to him?" Arthur took a minute, leaning back in his couch with his rum and Coke.

"Well, dear fellow... I'm afraid that's.., confidential; I will tell you he claims he's in good health, but that is all I can say at this time."

"Look, Arthur," I said, leaning on him a bit, "damn it, this is my family we're talking about. Did he leave a forwarding address?"

"Can't say, dear boy," he replied, pretending to be distracted and fidgeting with a piece of thread on the couch. This was maddening, but the old man was stubborn. I finally gave in and wished them good day. Kuo must have sworn them to secrecy also. Before I left, Arthur asked me if I was still practicing martial arts. He wagged his finger at me. "You know martial arts will keep you fit at any age."

Yeah, I thought, *look what it's done for you*. But I knew of at least one martial art which could deliver on this promise, the grand ultimate way of the fist, T'ai Chi Chuan.

All communication from my uncle ceased after his letter to the Fongs as far as I knew. Why we hadn't heard from him? Why was he being so mysterious, and what was it he felt needed to be concealed from us at all costs? Was he hurt? Did he need help? All these questions have been regrettably unanswered for me to this day. I undertook one last trip to Taiwan in 1970, following my mother's death. Exhaustive searches for Kuo through records and correspondence, including lengthy conversations with Taiwanese military officials, turned up nothing. After this, the trail went finally and completely cold. My more distant relatives had given him up for dead, but my mother held out hope that she would see him until her final days, and so did I.

An odd postscript to the affair came from none other than Ba Ling, who having discovered Kuo had been missing for some time, sent the family a letter of condolence, plunging us into further confusion. In the letter she mentioned a foreign exchange student of hers who claimed he was introduced by a group of monks to some "homeless looking guy they called a master" teaching T'ai Chi in the mountains of Taipei with over a thousand followers. According to Ba Ling, the student then proceeded to describe Uncle Kuo to a tee just as she remembered him. She said the student went on at length about the so called master being famous for putting novices through peculiar rituals and that Taiwanese authorities received hundreds of complaints, but he always managed to elude them. She said this didn't sound like Kuo, and that it was probably just a coincidence. I had to agree; this certainly didn't sound like him, although it could have offered one troubling explanation for his disappearance.

I xerox copied the letter in which Ba Ling sent her love, "Especially to Paulie," adding that she wished we could have established a closer relationship. Unfortunately, Constance found it after a bit of spring cleaning. She still brings it up first then gives me the silent treatment on occasion, bristling whenever she hears the name. Could I really explain to Constance what our so-called relationship was even about? Or what I would have sacrificed to get my hands on any bit of news about my uncle. "It's in the past...." I told my loving wife. "Leave it there."

Chapter 32

Groping through the darkness as stealthily as possible for a man in his late sixties, Kuo arrived at a grove of oak trees in the higher mountain elevations described to him by his relative in Taipei. A well manicured lawn with trimmed hedges and Crocuses surrounded the shabby brown building where his brother was supposedly being kept. Two rusty cars sat beneath a shack where the tin roof had begun to peel off. Worn out from a filthy bus ride and seven hours on foot, Kuo decided to make camp on the outskirts of the grove for the night and in the morning confront the people inside about his brother come what may. After unwrapping a wool blanket from his knapsack, Kuo found it impossible to get to sleep at first in his damp, uncomfortable surroundings but drifted off after what seemed like an eternity.

At dawn he was awakened by a dangerously sharp prodding below the ribs. Two men dressed in what he recognized to be Chinese soldiers' uniforms stood over him. Both carried bayoneted rifles, one of which was pointed right at his face. The two men had cigarettes dangling from their lips and were taking turns laughing at him. Once Kuo's eyes became accustomed to the morning gloom, he realized the soldier's uniforms were several years out of date and that the two goons standing over him were monks disguised as lookouts in old fashioned camouflage gear. He surmised their job was to patrol the perimeter of the dwelling where Kuo's brother was being kept or held. At that point, he was still unsure which.

He put a hand up to block the sunlight squeezed between the two men's heads. With a hoarse greeting out of his parched throat which sounded more like a grunt, Kuo attempted to communicate that he'd been looking all over the mountainside for his brother, that he was told by villagers he could be found here and pointed toward the building. The two men dragged Kuo to his feet. One of them gagged him while the other grabbed a handkerchief and started to tie Kuo's hands behind his back.

Minutes later both men exploded through the doorway of the building and landed flat on their faces in a cloud of dust. Kuo stood behind them, holding a cocked rifle in each hand. A flabby man wearing an apron, obviously a cook, dropped a huge cauldron he'd been carrying from the stove, splashed its contents all over the floor, and began yelling for help. Kuo held both rifles to his chest, telling him to shut up. Four men entered the room. Kuo swung one of the rifles toward them and they all put up their hands.

"I am Kuo Yun San!" he boomed over the commotion. "Where are you keeping my brother?" He suddenly fired a bullet into the wall over the lead man's head who held his hands higher and trembled in response.

"We are holy men! Please don't shoot us!"

"Not as holy as you might appear," replied Kuo sarcastically. The portly cook reached for a ladle behind his back and came at Kuo who promptly kicked it out of his hand. The cook crumpled on the floor moaning and clutching his injured hand.

"Enough!" cried a voice from one of the back rooms. "Everyone stand back! This is my brother, a T'ai Chi Chuan grandmaster; he could have killed you all by now if he wanted to!" There was a tense moment of silence in which you could hear individual drops of rainwater falling off the roof. Everyone in the room stayed motionless except for the cook who was still writhing on the floor, moaning in pain. The two monks dressed as soldiers who greeted Kuo continued lying on the ground unconscious, still as puppets.

Kuo's brother, obviously in no mood to give him a warm greeting either, was shouting. "What on earth are you doing here?" he demanded. "How did you..." But before he could finish his sentence, two other more imposing guards armed with Kalashnikov rifles and bulletproof vests burst through the front door. Kuo's brother held out both his arms to stop them, telling them to put down their weapons. "Everything's all right," he said.

"My brother's here... now we have to figure out what to do with him," he grumbled between clenched teeth.

"What happened over here?" asked one of the guards motioning to the two men on the floor with his rifle who were just beginning to regain consciousness. The other guard was already kneeling over them, feeling for a pulse.

"They will be fine in a few minutes," Kuo informed the one standing. "Make sure you give them some water when they wake up." Then lowering his voice, he asked his brother if there were somewhere they could talk in private. His brother nodded, instructing everyone to calm down and go about their business until he got back. He then ushered Kuo into one of the back rooms and closed the door. Slowly, the men began to relax their guard, and one of the monks rushed over to attend to the cook, carefully applying a poultice and wrapping his severely injured hand. The man was in such pain that tears ran continuously down his cheeks until nightfall.

Kuo's talk with his brother would turn into a major conversation which lasted most of afternoon and into the wee hours of the next day, interrupted only once by a monk who brought in tea along with two bowls of sour tasting beef stew and a plate of stale biscuits. Kuo's brother, referred to only as Abbot Chang, apologized for the fare but said what was he to do since Kuo had put the household cook out of commission, possibly for the duration of the week. Kuo returned the apology, saying what was he to do since the man was about to attack him with a cooking utensil. Both men smiled, got up, and gave each other a lingering hug. From there Kuo launched into a lengthy tale about his stay in New York, the T'ai Chi school, his involvement with the Chen family, his two nephews and his divorce from a woman he almost wound up with.

As the light changed through a pair of drawn curtains, he could see that his brother was growing pale, that his eyes were hazy, and that his face reflected a greenish pallor. When Kuo hugged him, his ribcage felt like a bundle of dried leaves. Noticing the concern on Kuo's face, Chang revealed that the local doctors had given up on him, told him he had stage four pancreatic cancer and only a few months to live, if that. Nothing more could be done, he said, though he had exhausted every available resource to him including the help of some local homeopathic healers. Kuo gripped his brother by the arm attempting to convince him that he had experienced a great deal of success in the area of healing people mentally and physically by directing the pathways of their chi and using other techniques taught to him before he left China, but his brother shook his head. Again he reiterated to Kuo that his condition was so permanently serious that it could never be reversed, even by the most experienced of holistic and homeopathic practitioners. He was simply going to die and was forced to accept the fact some time ago. Chang steered the conversation away from his failing health, seemingly unfazed, as if he had something more important to discuss than his own death.

"Continue, brother Kuo, where have you been and what have you been up to all these years?" Chang listened patiently for several hours to his brother's account of his stay in New York, fraught with all its many encounters and adventures, including a description of his two nephews, whom he considered family treasures. Afterward, Chang rose unsteadily to his feet and began pacing the room with one hand covering his mouth, deep in thought.

"You may have entered our lives at a very opportune moment," he said at last, resuming his seat. "I started a school here some time ago for a few illegitimate sons of the monks. They were treated as outcasts in the public schools, and I couldn't have that. When it started, I was full of energy, but now some of them need a strong hand, and they wear me out daily. We could use your help," he admitted, looking at Kuo pleadingly through yellow eyeballs.

Kuo instantly accepted. He had been searching for some way to help his brother, and now it had been handed to him. He had no way of knowing that acceding to his brother's request would prove disastrous. Looking ostensibly relieved, Abbot Chang continued.

"There is one area in which you could be of particular help to me," he continued with a look of deep concern. "We have a student here from America, the son of a diplomat who has recently taken up residence in Taipei." Abbot Chang let out a deep, troubled sigh. "His father sent him to live with us in hopes that he might learn some ethical principles by example from our way of life. Trouble is, I myself am on the run from the law because of bad debts, and the boy has found me out. He is full of hatred for all of us, including his mother and father who have recently separated. He has caused us nothing but trouble since he came here and stirred up much bitterness among people in the monastic order. Just as I was about to send him packing back to his father, I receive a draft notice in the mail yesterday saying he would have to return to the U.S. in two months to ship out or face prosecution along with a polite note from his father refusing to take him back. I suppose I have developed a soft spot for the kid, despite his malicious and disobedient ways, but I don't want him going off to war with a bad taste in his mouth about the time he spent here. He was my responsibility after all, placed here under my care and tutelage."

Kuo shrugged, listening to all this. "What is it you think I can do?" he asked.

"You have been spending time getting to know American culture," replied Chang. "You know how they think and feel, what is popular to them, their likes and dislikes, hopes and dreams. You may be able to reach this kid in ways that aren't possible for me. At any rate, I wish you would give it a try. He keeps bragging about a Karate school his family sent him to in America which taught him a bunch of nonsense, but he swears by it either from pride or ignorance. The monks routinely thrash him up one side of the mountain and down the other and he has come back with his face bloody but refuses to let them teach him anything because he doesn't trust or respect them. Same goes for the other children. Anyway, I want you to teach him and the other kids the art of Kung Fu, specifically T'ai Chi Chuan, the proper way for self-defence."

Kuo looked at him intently. "If this boy, as you call him, doesn't obey you, what makes you think he will obey me?" he asked.

"For the reasons I've just described," responded Chang. "In addition, you have an air of authority about you that people seem to respect, unlike the monks and others around here. I have a room you can stay in and..."

Kuo interrupted him. "Well I'm not so sure I'll be staying here."

"It is the only way." Abbot Chang's tone became irritable and impatient as often happens with a man who has only a short time to live. "Besides, it is my dying wish, and I want you to start now...tomorrow." Kuo sipped his tea and said nothing.

Chapter 33

From their very first encounter, the American diplomat's son hated Kuo, biting his lip to contain his rage anytime they came within close proximity of each other. In fact, his dislike of Kuo was so intense that he couldn't even bring himself to look him in the face. He developed an irritating habit of turning away from the master whenever he was being addressed. Kuo, used to the enormous respect bordering on subservience he received from his American students, was frustrated with him immediately. Try as he might, regaling him with stories about America which the student walked out on before he could finish, Kuo never did succeeded in breaking the ice with this most stubborn of apprentices. To his credit, the student was more or less obedient when it came to the punishing training Kuo routinely put the students through, but Kuo believed this was more a result of empathy with the novice monks than out of any respect for him.

Kuo fluctuated between elation and despair at his new task but threw himself into it. He hated his tiny living quarters, about the size of a bathroom in the West, and the uncomfortable, filthy cot he slept in; although these and the fact that he had a private room in which to sleep were considered immense luxuries in Taiwan. On a positive note, thanks to Abbot Chang's new directive, the guards treated him with respect, and he even managed to befriend the cook, introducing him to recipes he felt would prove more nutritious. Day after day, he battled an avalanche of memories about New York, his American family, the school, his divorce, and the fact that he wouldn't be able to attend Paulie's wedding as he had faithfully promised. Most heartbreaking of all were the attempts to get word to them while fighting to keep his identity and whereabouts a secret. Dozens of letters sent to America through the monks and emissaries never reached their destination. Practically all were intercepted and divested of their postage stamps, used to barter for food and household sundries. Phone calls overseas could also be tricky. My uncle was suspicious of phones, especially in Taiwan or China, and fearful of making any calls he felt could be traced.

Every morning Kuo got up at four a.m., ate a quick breakfast of congi or rice gruel and tea which he prepared for himself and some of the boys. Then he rose from the table and clapped his hands twice, the signal for the boys to rush outside and get in formation, after which they faced a training regimen which took up the majority of their day. Kuo smiled to himself in amusement when he thought of the words his brother used about the students "needing a strong hand." *That's exactly what they'll get,* he thought, and Kuo knew about such things. He had them jumping up flights of stairs on all fours like grasshoppers, pounding trunks of trees with their fists repeatedly until pieces of bark flew off, hanging for hours upside down with their feet strapped between two poles, or running shirtless in freezing cold weather for the same amount of time. He made them smash their palms for days on end into pots filled with metal filings and then stand in silent meditation until one or more of them passed out from the searing pain in their joints.

Fa and I suffered through a couple of these practices but were thankfully spared most of what the poor monks under his barbarous instruction were later forced to endure. Without boundaries and left to his own devices, Kuo dreamed up his own personal tortuous routines for the hapless monks which to some defied logic. The few who witnessed them expressed concern to the monastic order that they felt the great master Kuo was becoming senile.

Of course, Kuo knew exactly what he was doing, toughening them up Shaolin style with training combinations only true masters knew about or were able to improvise without causing physical harm to their understudies. Once word leaked out that the famous master was training students up in the mountains, a great many started to brave the rough terrain in order to make a pilgrimage, either just to see him or be in his presence. Over a period of weeks, hundreds of aspiring devotees, most of whom were turned away, could be found camping all over the mountainside. Kuo became concerned. He knew it wouldn't be long before Taiwanese officials followed, possibly bringing swat teams looking for his brother.

His worst fears were realized one freezing morning in November. Kuo had been in residence almost two months. A group of Taiwanese military police surrounded the compound and proceeded to knock repeatedly and impatiently at the front door. Some who heard rustling and voices of the men outside managed to slip away beneath the cover of mountain underbrush. Kuo and Chang were both shot with rifles at point black range where they slept. The American student managed to escape but recklessly came back to see if Kuo was still alive or if he could remove anything from his person to prove whom he'd been studying with.

Abbot Chang had been dead for hours. Kuo hung on, barely breathing with eyes wide open. When he saw the American student had come back he weakly beckoned to him. Kuo grabbed the boy by the shirt collar, pulling him in close. "Your life is in danger!" he hissed. Listen...I need a favour. When you get back stateside look up the 'Kuo Yun San School of T'ai Chi Chuan' in Chinatown, New York City, and give this to a man named Paul Chen! Understand?" he asked, grabbing even more furiously at the boy's shirt. The boy nodded in reply. Kuo drew a sword from behind his back sheathed in a scabbard with some writing on it and crammed an envelope down inside the scabbard as far as it would go. Then he handed it over to the student and slipped into unconsciousness. Soon afterward, the student heard unfamiliar voices outside but again managed to make a clean getaway.

Two soldiers were shovelling dirt and lime over the bodies of Kuo and Abbot Chang for whom they were digging unmarked graves on a mountain slope. One of them piped up "Hey, I know this guy, wasn't he supposed to be a really tough Kung Fu master or something? Pretty famous too, as I recall."

The other put a cigarette out in Kuo's grave and shovelled another load of earth on top of it, then remarked" Yeah well, he doesn't look so tough now."

At approximately the same time that Kuo was being buried, the American son of a diplomat stood at the edge of a mountain precipice. He hated his teacher Kuo so much that he wound up agonizing long and hard about whether to hurl the sword and its contents over the cliff. At the last moment, he decided to keep it. Perhaps he would try to sell it at a novelty shop when he got back to the States or hang on to it as a trophy to impress his friends. Fulfilling Kuo's dying wish was the farthest thing from his mind at the time, though in the end, he would wind up doing just that. He would have laughed if you told him what the Viet Minh foot soldier had in store for him, or that he would be awarded the posthumous Medal of Honour for bravery in combat.

Chapter 34

Thoughts flickered and disappeared inside my head like dying embers. I catch myself staring at the horizon from a suite of offices on the fifty seventh floor, overlooking Central Park. I'd been sitting back in one of the office chairs with an empty cut crystal scotch glass in hand, waiting for my partner to arrive so we could go over the brief I started at six this morning. I felt the building shudder a little from the corporate helicopter landing on the roofs helipad.

Minutes later, my partner, Jeff, had come bounding in with a briefcase in each hand. "Oh great, you're here," he said, panting happily. "The deal went through you know?...with the Chinese. Hey, what's wrong; why the long face?" After a quick pause he snapped his fingers. "It's your Uncle's birthday isn't it? Sorry Paul, I should have gotten him a present, I know, but at least I brought you one," he quipped.

I pulled the brief I prepared out of a drawer and handed it to him. "Look Jeff," I said. The evening and the scotch were beginning to take their toll. "I have to get out of here and go home to the wife and kids, you know how it is."

"Sure Paul," he said. "Have a great weekend...and cheer up will you?" he called after me, but I'd already closed the door.

Chapter 35

Two precious items are cared for meticulously in a safe, the combination of which is known only to myself and my immediate family. They dwell high above the city in a block of penthouse office suites, and I'm thinking of them now as I stand by one of the windows overlooking Central Park. I had been teaching my Uncle's T'ai Chi as a hobby for some time and temporarily confiscated them years ago from a student who was repeatedly late for class and bragged that he'd been taught by a famous master who's name he wouldn't reveal. Though I was fully prepared to return the items and speak to the student about them, he was drafted to Vietnam that same week, and I never saw him again. I was later told by relatives he'd been listed as missing in action. The entire time I've clung to these items, there wasn't even a notion of returning them to his family because I felt so strongly they belonged to mine. A chill goes down my spine whenever I think of the steps it took for them to come into my possession. One of them was carefully hidden inside the other.

I made the discovery one day while teaching a class. The student I mentioned always brought an interesting sword to class which seemed to have small but familiar Chinese lettering on the scabbard I could never quite make out. Once, when he was in the bathroom, I peaked inside his sword bag. While I couldn't be sure at that moment, I could have sworn I saw the name Kuo Yun San engraved on the scabbard in small Chinese characters. As I tilted the bag to close it, a parchment like piece of paper fell on the floor. I hurriedly stuffed it back in the bag but after the items had been left in my care, so to speak, I suddenly remembered it. What I discovered was indeed a scabbard with the name Kuo Yun San clearly engraved on it in red Chinese characters. I also discovered a letter in an envelope, dated June 1940, that read:

Dearest Kuo Yun San,

Thank you from the bottom of our hearts for all you have done. Thank you most of all for being my protection and faithful companion during the time we travelled in the United States. We will personally never forget your great kindness and impeccable service to us.

Gratefully,

Mme. Chiang Kai Shek.

The final sentence was typed with a completely illegible signature scribbled below it. Below that was a red stamped government seal. I smiled when I read this for the first time. Beneath everything lay my uncle's true colours, duty and servitude to the last.

We would like to thank you, the reader,
for purchasing this book.

We hope you have enjoyed it as much as we have!

CPSIA information can be obtained at www.ICGtesting.com
Printed in the USA
BVOW03s1843260215

389522BV00002B/126/P